Footste...

It wasn't ~~~~~~~~~~~~ they had no one staying at the hotel at the moment. Maybe this was someone who wanted to book a room. Tina turned with a welcoming smile.

That smile died on her lips when she saw the cowboy standing in front of her.

Cole Slater.

In one startled, reflexive sweep, she took in almost everything about him. The light brown hair showing beneath the brim of his battered hat. The firm mouth and jaw. Broad shoulders. Narrow hips. The well-worn jeans, silver belt buckle and scuffed boots. In the next reluctant second, she turned her gaze to the one feature she had deliberately skipped over the first time.

A pair of blue eyes that made her think instantly of her son.

She clutched the grocery sack and demanded, "What are you doing here?"

His face looked flushed. But he didn't look angry, the way he would have if he'd seen Robbie and put two and two together. She breathed a sigh of relief at the reprieve, no matter how brief, giving her a chance to come to grips with his reappearance.

If she ever could.

Dear Reader,

Cowboy Creek is typical of my small towns, where everyone knows everyone else—and their business. Though you'll find lots of matchmakers and nosy neighbors around, you can be sure they're all wonderful folks at heart.

No one in Cowboy Creek has a bigger heart than Jed Garland, the local hotel owner and meddling grandpa who wants to see his granddaughters happy and settled down. Oh...and providing him with a few more great-grandchildren!

In *The Cowboy's Little Surprise*, I hope you enjoy discovering how a marriage-shy cowboy handles secrets, betrayal, unexpected fatherhood and a matchmaker who is certain he knows what's best for him.

As always, I would love to hear what you think about this story. You can reach me at PO Box 504, Gilbert, AZ 85299, or through my website, barbarawhitedaille.com. You can also find me on Facebook (barbarawhitedaille) and Twitter, @BarbaraWDaille.

All my best to you.

Until we meet again,

Barbara White Daille

THE COWBOY'S LITTLE SURPRISE

BARBARA WHITE DAILLE

HARLEQUIN® AMERICAN ROMANCE®

If you purchased this book without a cover you should be aware that this book is stolen property. It was reported as "unsold and destroyed" to the publisher, and neither the author nor the publisher has received any payment for this "stripped book."

Recycling programs
for this product may
not exist in your area.

ISBN-13: 978-0-373-75564-6

The Cowboy's Little Surprise

Copyright © 2015 by BARBARA WHITE-RAYCZEK

All rights reserved. Except for use in any review, the reproduction or utilization of this work in whole or in part in any form by any electronic, mechanical or other means, now known or hereinafter invented, including xerography, photocopying and recording, or in any information storage or retrieval system, is forbidden without the written permission of the publisher, Harlequin Enterprises Limited, 225 Duncan Mill Road, Don Mills, Ontario M3B 3K9, Canada.

This is a work of fiction. Names, characters, places and incidents are either the product of the author's imagination or are used fictitiously, and any resemblance to actual persons, living or dead, business establishments, events or locales is entirely coincidental.

This edition published by arrangement with Harlequin Books S.A.

For questions and comments about the quality of this book, please contact us at CustomerService@Harlequin.com.

® and TM are trademarks of Harlequin Enterprises Limited or its corporate affiliates. Trademarks indicated with ® are registered in the United States Patent and Trademark Office, the Canadian Intellectual Property Office and in other countries.

Printed in U.S.A.

Barbara White Daille lives with her husband in the sunny Southwest, where they don't mind the lizards in their front yard but could do without the scorpions in the bathroom.

A writer from the age of nine and a novelist since eighth grade, Barbara is now an award-winning author with a number of novels to her credit.

When she was very young, Barbara learned from her mom about the storytelling magic in books—and she's been hooked ever since. She hopes you will enjoy reading her books and will find your own magic in them!

She'd also love to have you drop by and visit with her at her website, barbarawhitedaille.com.

Books by Barbara White Daille

HARLEQUIN AMERICAN ROMANCE

The Sheriff's Son
Court Me, Cowboy
Family Matters
A Rancher's Pride
The Rodeo Man's Daughter
Honorable Rancher
Rancher at Risk

Texas Rodeo Barons

The Texan's Little Secret

Visit the Author Profile page
at Harlequin.com for more titles

This book is dedicated only, and as always, to Rich.
I'm so glad we got hitched!

Prologue

Seventy-some-odd years on this earth had taught Jedediah Garland what made life most worth living—and it was the one thing he wanted more of to call his own. Not property. He owned plenty of that, between the Hitching Post Hotel and the ranch it sat on. Not friends. He had a sufficient number of those, too, and wouldn't give up a single one of them. But the most important thing...*family*.

That's where his life fell far short.

Paz came into the dining room toting his breakfast. The hotel business had quieted down some lately—heck, it had up and gone to Tahiti—and he and his cook had the room to themselves. She set the platter on the table in front of him.

"Chile relleno okay with you for tonight, boss?"

He shrugged.

She put her hands on her hips. "What? All of a sudden you don't like what I make for you?"

"It's not that." He shifted the cutlery on his napkin. "I'm off my feed today. It's Thom's birthday."

"Yes."

He thought of his eldest son, now long gone, and the rest of his small family, mostly scattered across the country. "I never thought things would come to pass the way they have. And I don't know what I would do without you and Tina here."

His youngest granddaughter was also Paz's only grandchild. Tina and her four-year-old son were the only members of his family to live under his roof. "You know, Mary and I always thought we'd have our kids around us, if not on the ranch, then at least settled somewhere within hailing distance of Cowboy Creek. And we'd expected to see all the grandkids growing up in the area."

"Yes, I know. But the girls plan to visit. You can spend time with them soon."

"A week? Two weeks? That's not enough." He slapped his palm on the table. "And if the granddaughters I've got are all I'm going to have—well, I'll learn to live with that. But they need to get busy and give us more great-grandkids. Heck, they all need to get married. Besides..." Frowning, he resettled the napkin beneath the cutlery at his place. After a long moment, he muttered, "I don't like seeing my girls unhappy."

"You think they're not happy?"

"Of course they're not. How can they be? One's traipsing all over the world with not a chance of settling down. Another's trying to raise two kids by herself. And then there's Tina, on her own with Robbie. You want her married, too, don't you?"

"Yes. But Tina's very proud..."

"And we're proud of her." His youngest granddaughter had studied hard in school, then gone on to get her degrees. Now she kept the books for him and helped manage the hotel. Yes, they were both so proud of her.

Paz stared down at the tabletop.

He frowned. "I know what you're thinking, and *you* know it makes no difference to me that our kids never got married. Tina's just as much my granddaughter as Jane and Andi are."

"Yes, I do know that."

"Then tell me, flat-out straight, what's bugging you?"

"Tina. She's so independent."

"Yeah. Too independent for her own good. Something's got to be done about her, Paz. About her and my granddaughters, too."

She said nothing.

He sighed and rubbed his chin. The rasp of a few whiskers he'd missed shaving that morning sounded loud in the silence. "I stopped in at SugarPie's the other day." Sugar Conway ran a combination bakery / sandwich shop / gossip parlor in the center of Cowboy Creek. "Sugar didn't have any details yet, but the word is, Cole Slater may be headed back to town."

Paz dropped the serving tray, which knocked against the saltshaker, spewing salt across the bare wooden tabletop. "Oh, I'm sorry, boss." With hurried, jerky movements, she brushed the loose salt into her palm.

He frowned. "Something wrong?"

"No. Why should there be anything wrong?"

But she didn't meet his gaze. He frowned at her bent head and eyed the silver strands threaded through her once-dark hair. Paz had worked for him for twenty years and more, and he could spot something odd about her with his eyes closed. "It's not like you to drop things in the dining room. Or the kitchen or anywhere else for that matter."

"I'm just rushing because I'm running late."

He eyed her. "No later than normal. So I'll ask you again, what's up?"

"I was speaking with Sugar this morning," she said with obvious reluctance.

"Must be some good scandal flying around to warrant

a call this early." He sat back in his chair without asking for details, knowing full well Paz would fill him in. And why not? As one of the town's business owners, he had a right to know what happened in Cowboy Creek.

"Sugar said Layne just confirmed it this morning," Paz said in a low tone. "Her brother will be here next week."

"Will he? Well, it's about time. It's—what?—five years now he's been gone." He'd thrown that last comment out offhandedly, but to tell the truth, he knew down to the hour when Cole Slater had left town. "It seems to me Tina mentioned his name quite a bit in their school days."

"Because their teachers had them work together."

"Right. Now you say that, I do recall. And now he's coming back, I've had another idea. There's no reason those two shouldn't work together again."

"Oh, boss, I don't think…"

"There's nothing you *need* to think about. This idea's got some strong possibilities, too, and I'm just the man to put it in place." He smiled. "Don't you worry, Paz. None of these kids will have a clue as to what's going on."

Chapter One

Two weeks later

To Cole Slater, walking into the Hitching Post Hotel felt like coming home…which probably didn't mean much, considering he'd hated the home he had grown up in and hadn't stayed in any one place since leaving it.

He stared around him in awe. Everything looked the same as it had the day he'd shown up here as a high-school senior, as raw as any wrangler could have been, to start a job on Garland Ranch. In those early days, he'd ridden the line between a determination to prove himself and the stomach-clenching certainty he was in way over his head.

Exactly the way he'd felt since his return to Cowboy Creek.

Pushing the thought aside, he turned to Jed, who hadn't changed much, either. His white hair was combed neatly into place, as always, and he wore the same string tie and belt buckle Cole had never seen him without.

"Glad you could drop by," his former boss said.

"I appreciate the invitation. As the saying goes, you're not looking a day older, Jed. And things around here don't seem to have changed a bit."

Jed beamed. "We try to keep the place up."

"You've done a good job of it."

Years of polishing had buffed the hotel's registration desk to a high sheen. The brass foot rail encircling it gleamed. Even the knotty-pine walls and flooring of the reception area gave off a soft glow, as if the candles in the wrought-iron holders on the wall had been set to flame.

In the sitting room off to one side of the entry, the same heavy, low-slung couches and chairs sported the same handmade afghans, and the chime clock on the wall still ticked the seconds away like a slow, steady heartbeat.

Or maybe that was his own heart, thumping so hard he could hear it.

No, the Hitching Post hadn't changed. Neither had the old man in front of him. But he himself sure had, and the time had come for him to prove it.

"Paz and Tina will be sorry they missed you."

At the statement, he froze. Jed couldn't know just how wrong he'd been. Paz, yeah, maybe she would be happy to see him again, and he felt the same. But Tina...

He'd practically grown up with Jed's granddaughter. They'd had the same teachers all through the lower grades and even shared some of the same classes in high school. But after what had happened between them senior year, Tina would never want to see him again.

"C'mon back." Jed waved at him to follow and walked away.

Cole knew where they were headed. From his days of working here, he knew the ranch and the hotel well. Halfway along the hall, he stopped in the doorway of the small, overcrowded den where Jed would sit every Friday when his men came to collect their pay. On a good many of those Friday nights, Cole would hang around to talk to the boss long after the rest of the wranglers had left.

The old man probably still handled his payroll from

here. He had always claimed the den was the only danged room in the hotel he could call his own.

Now his former boss took a seat in the leather chair behind the massive handmade desk. He rested his gnarled fists on its surface, looked at Cole and said not a word.

Cole stepped into the den and swung the door closed behind him.

Jed waved toward one of the guest chairs. "Never thought I'd see you sitting in front of me at this desk again."

"Me, either. I owe you an apology, Jed."

"Do you, now?"

"You know I do. For leaving here without letting you know I planned to quit."

"That *was* a surprise, I'll admit. Walking off without notice happens with cowhands who move around. I see that go on all the time. It's not what I'd expect from a man I keep on the payroll. And then, never to hear a word..."

"Yeah." He ran his thumb along the arm of the chair. "I've been on the move."

"On the run."

He froze.

"And, I take it," Jed continued, "by nobody's choice but your own."

"It didn't exactly happen like that." He sighed. "I just wanted to get out of Cowboy Creek. You know once I was left as Layne's legal guardian, our lives got a little crazy."

"All the more reason to reach out to a friend."

"I couldn't do that. Not again." He shrugged, as if he could dislodge the burden he'd carried since that time. He was just turned eighteen and caring for his younger sister on his own. Their mama had recently died and their dad had passed on a couple of years before that. His boss had known all this back then.

"I never wanted to ask you for those advances to my

pay. But Layne was still trying to deal with losing Mama when her boyfriend dumped her—on her sixteenth birthday. She was a mess." He shook his head. "I wanted to get her something special. Heck, I wanted to buy food to put in our fridge. But all my pay had already gone to the rent."

Sitting back in his chair, Jed laced his fingers across his belly and squinted again. "At least you had your head on straight about your sister. I'll give you that. Family's important." He sounded more sad than angry now. But he frowned. "Why the hell didn't you tell me back then you still needed help, boy?"

Cole took a deep breath and gestured uselessly. What could he have said? That he wanted to keep Jed's respect for stepping up and taking care of his own? That he hated the thought of admitting his helplessness to the man he looked up to more than he ever had to his own dad?

Instead, unable to say either of those things and worried nearly to death about Layne, he'd turned around and betrayed the one person who'd believed in him.

"Anyhow," he said, "once she and her boyfriend made up, she wanted to get married. She was underage, and as her guardian, she needed me to sign the paperwork to give my okay. And I did." He sighed. "I didn't stop to think about much else. I was still just a kid myself, too dumb to know that walking away from a job without notice wasn't the right thing to do. But all I could see was that getting Layne settled gave me my ticket out. So I grabbed it and never looked back. Now, she's on her own again, only this time she's got both a kid *and* one on the way. So here I am." He took a deep breath. "I always intended to apologize to you. And to pay back the advances."

The old man's white eyebrows shot up. "It's sure taken you a while to get around to it."

"I know that, too. This is the first time I've come back to

town since then." For one reason or a dozen, none of which he wanted to think about. "It didn't sit right for me to just mail you a check. When I paid my obligation, I wanted to make sure I was looking you in the eye."

"Folks say a handshake between friends is worth its weight in gold." Jed stood and reached across the desk. When they clasped hands, the old man's grip was as strong and sure as it had ever been.

"And I need to take care of those advances." He pulled out his wallet. "No haggling over this, Jed. I owe you."

"Well, we can let that part go."

Cole frowned. He didn't want their conversation to end this way. After all this time, he wanted to pay his debt in full. To finally get rid of the burden. But Jed, jaw set stubbornly, had returned to his seat.

Instead of the redemption he'd hoped for, he would have to settle temporarily for that handshake and the knowledge he hadn't lost a friend.

"I *have* got a proposition for you, though," Jed said. "Now you're back in town, you'll need a job."

"Yeah. I figure I'll get picked up at one of the ranches around here, even if it's just through the summer."

"I want you on this ranch."

"Here?"

Jed laughed. "Don't sound so surprised. You worked out fine the first time, didn't you?"

He had to take another long breath before he would trust his voice again. "We just went through this. I walked away. And you went five years without hearing from me, without me paying my debt. Yet you want to hire me on again?"

"Are you listening to what you're saying, boy? That's three loads of guilt in one sentence. Sounds like you'd darned well better take this offer if you're ever gonna get over yourself."

Cole shook his head. His old boss always had read him better than anyone could.

"I'll wager Pete will be happy to see you again."

Surprised, Cole said, "Pete Brannigan?" The man had broken him in during his early days on the ranch. He'd felt sure Pete, a few years older, would have moved on by this time. "He's still wrangling for you?"

"That and more. He's managing the place for me now. Lives right here on the ranch with his family. And he's been saying we could use an extra hand. So, what do you say?"

He hesitated, though he knew full well he'd have to take the offer. He needed a steady job. This one would give him a chance to prove to Jed he'd changed. At the same time, it might give him an idea of how to pay the man back.

But it would also put him in danger of running into Tina. Tina...who, with one short conversation with her granddaddy, could get him thrown off Garland Ranch.

TINA PULLED THE ranch's truck into the empty parking lot behind the Hitching Post. As she and her grandmother climbed out of the cab, she said, "Abuela, you go ahead in with the frozen food, and I'll take care of the rest."

"You can handle all that?"

"Sure," she said. "This is nothing."

And that was a problem.

The small size of their order from the Local-General Store reflected the lack of guests at the hotel. As the hotel's bookkeeper, she found that lack giving her plenty to worry about lately. Sure, it was only early March, never one of their busiest seasons, but it was quieter than usual for this time of year. Their bookings for the summer hadn't begun to pick up yet, either.

"We'll need to go back to the store again soon, before Jane and Andi arrive."

"No problem, Abuela. I know you need to buy everything fresh. John Barrett must love seeing us walk into the L-G so often."

"I think you're right."

John had established the market forty years ago, naming it the Local-General Store. He claimed building it smack in the middle of Cowboy Creek made it local to everybody, and stocking everything under the sun made it general. The store's popularity—despite the attempt of a couple of national chains to take over—seemed to have proven him right.

She looked over at Abuela, who was still gathering the couple of insulated carrier bags she used for frozen food.

"Is everything okay? You've been looking tired lately." More than tired. Her shoulders seemed slightly stooped, the lines under her eyes more pronounced. With her grandparents always so active, Tina sometimes had to remind herself they'd both reached their seventies. "Has Robbie been wearing you out? He's got so much energy."

"Don't be silly. And a four-year-old must have lots of energy."

It wasn't till Abuela was halfway up the steps of the hotel that Tina realized she hadn't answered the first question. *Was* everything okay with her? Was she concerned about Jed, the way Tina had been for a while now?

Though she hadn't learned she was Jed's granddaughter until shortly before she had started school, he had always been her *abuelo*. She loved him just as much as she loved Robbie and Abuela.

His behavior lately had her very concerned. He'd been acting odd, distracted, as if he were worried about something. But of course, there was one perfectly logical reason for that. He had the same worries she did.

Ever since high school, she had helped keep the hotel's books for Jed. Very early on, she had learned that when people were forced to budget, vacation funds often went in the first cut. And the Hitching Post felt the pain. That meant she felt the pain, as well. She glanced up at the hotel, all three stories of it, all the way up to the windows of her attic hideaway. She loved the hotel, the only home she and Robbie had ever known. Jed, who had also lived here all of his life, couldn't like the idea of all those empty rooms, either.

Sighing, she reached for one of the grocery sacks in the back of the truck. Footsteps on gravel made her pause. It wasn't Jed's familiar tread, and they had no one staying at the hotel at the moment. Maybe this was someone who wanted to book a room. She turned with a welcoming smile.

That smile died on her lips when she saw the cowboy standing in front of her.

Cole Slater.

In one startled, reflexive sweep, she took in almost everything about him. The light brown hair showing beneath the brim of his battered hat. The firm mouth and jaw. Broad shoulders. Narrow hips. The well-worn jeans, silver belt buckle, and scuffed boots. In the next reluctant second, she turned her gaze to the one feature she had deliberately skipped over the first time.

A pair of blue eyes that made her think instantly of her son.

Clutching the grocery sack, she demanded, "What are you doing here?"

His face looked flushed. But he didn't appear angry, the way he would have if he'd seen Robbie and put two and two together. She breathed a sigh of relief at the reprieve, no matter how brief, giving her a chance to come to grips with his return to town. If she ever could.

Seeing him again had brought back years of memories she didn't want to think about.

She should have known better than to fall for Cole Slater. At the tender age of seven, she had already heard about his reputation as a sweet-talker. By junior high, he had progressed to a real player. And by senior high, he had turned love-'em-and-leave-'em into an art form, changing girlfriends as often as she replaced guest towels here at the Hitching Post.

Too bad she hadn't remembered all that when he had finally turned his attention her way.

He shoved his hands into his back pockets, which pulled his shirt taut against his chest. Now, she felt herself flushing as she recalled the one and only time—

No, she wasn't going there. And he wasn't staying here. "You must have made a wrong turn somewhere. I suggest you find your vehicle, wherever you might have left it—"

"I parked near the barn—"

"—and be on your way."

"—and to answer your question, I came to see Jed."

"What for?"

"He invited me."

"Then I assume you've seen him already and, as I said, you can be on your way."

"You and I need to have something out first."

Please, no. Had he caught a glimpse of Robbie, after all?

He shifted his stance and crossed his arms over his chest. "I didn't expect to run into you this soon, but since we've met up, it's as good a time as any to talk."

"I don't really have anything to say to you."

"But I've got something to say to you."

He ducked his head, looking suddenly like the kindergartner made to give back the lollipop he'd just sweet-talked out of her hand. Even in those days, she'd have given him anything.

One night in high school, she'd proven that.

She turned to the truck and grabbed another sack. "I'm busy, sorry."

"I'll give you a hand, and then we can talk."

"No." He had stepped up beside her and stood only a few inches away. His nearness unsettled her. The thought of him going back into the hotel upset her even more.

While she and Abuela had been in town, her son had stayed over at the ranch manager's house on the property. But Pete's housekeeper might be bringing Robbie back home any minute.

"All right," she conceded. "Say whatever you want to say right here."

"I'm sorry."

She blinked. "What?"

He ducked his head again, then tugged the brim of his hat down, shading his eyes. "Look, I know I acted like a real jerk to you back in high school."

"High school? You mean that lunchtime you turned me down when I asked you to the dance?" *The time you humiliated me in front of everyone in the school cafeteria?* "I'm over that."

"You are?"

"Of course."

"Well. That's good. But I still feel I owe you an apology."

"Oh, please. Don't even think twice about it."

"You're sure?"

"Yes, I'm sure." She forced a smile and hoped he couldn't see her grinding her teeth in frustration. She just wanted him gone. Off the ranch. Anywhere but right here, right now.

"Well, that's good," he said again. "I'm glad you're not holding any bad feelings against me, since we'll probably be seeing a lot of each other."

"I doubt it. The hotel keeps me busy and close to home. I don't go into town much."

"You won't have to." His smile didn't look the least bit forced. "You'll see me here. I'm back to working for Jed."

Chapter Two

"Men are more trouble than they're worth."

Tina's best friend couldn't possibly know how much Tina agreed with the familiar refrain right at that moment.

She looked down the length of Canyon Road, Cowboy Creek's business section, then back at Ally. They had just met in the parking lot of the hardware store, where Ally worked as a clerk. As often as Tina could manage, they would get together at the end of Ally's workday to walk, pacing the length of the business section of Canyon Road and back again, for as long as their time allowed.

Right now, just a few hours after her meeting with Cole, she needed a good, long walk to work off her sky-high stress. And listening to Ally's complaints about the latest man in her life would be a good distraction. "What now, Al?"

"Oh, that new wrangler in town, the one I told you about—you know, the cute one."

"They're all cute to you. Can you be more specific?"

"Details. Always, you want details." Ally rolled her eyes. "The tall blond one who just showed up in town a week ago. He's been coming into the store a lot. But I can't get him to look my way. And you know I can be pretty hard to miss."

That was an understatement. Ally was nothing if not

flamboyant. Today after work she had changed into a magenta exercise leotard paired with electric-blue biker shorts and her favorite purple running shoes.

Tina wore her navy sweatpants and her faded New Mexico State University T-shirt.

Ally looked her up and down and shook her head. "When are you going to listen to me, *chica*?" she demanded.

"Don't start."

"Too late for that. I started on you years ago. I don't know why I love you when you're so darned stubborn."

"For my *abuela*'s Sopapilla cheesecake."

Ally laughed. "You've got a point."

"And as usual, my point right now would be that—as sorry as I am about your cute wrangler—you can't throw yourself at every good-looking cowhand who walks in. Please tell me you didn't do that with this one."

"I can't help my impetuous nature." Ally grinned. "You could learn something from me, *chica*. How to have your heart broken on a weekly basis. It would sure make your life more exciting."

"Once was enough for that, thanks," she said grimly.

Ally frowned. "You're not looking too happy yourself. What's wrong?"

She hesitated. But Ally was the only friend who could understand what Cole's return meant to her. "Your blond isn't the only man who's shown up in town. Cole's back."

"You're kidding me!"

Her best friend was also the only woman Tina knew who could manage to screech in a whisper.

"Do I look like I'm kidding?"

Ally shook her head, sending her dark curls tumbling around her shoulders. "No. You look like you're in shock. C'mon, let's get going."

Tina moved through the parking lot and out onto the sidewalk on autopilot, in the same manner she had gotten herself to the store. Somehow, she had made it all the way here without thinking again of Cole. Blurting out the news of his return to Ally had brought him back to her again.

A ridiculous choice of words, since he'd never been *hers* to begin with.

All through the years, despite his reputation, she saw glimpses of a Cole no one else knew. Or so she'd thought. Those glimpses gave her just enough hope for him. For her. Just enough reason to keep her crush alive.

But years of love from afar didn't equal a real relationship.

"How long is he going to be in town?" Ally demanded.

"I don't know."

"Well, we need to find out. And then you need to stay away from him. Hang out at the ranch, that's all, like you usually do. And keep Robbie with you."

"I can't hide from the man, Ally."

"Who's saying hide? But Cole doesn't deserve to know the truth. Not when he hasn't even bothered to send you a postcard in all this time."

All this time.

Five long years.

Ally shook her head. "After what he did, I can't believe you'll tell him anything."

What Cole had done to her that lunchtime had been bad, but what she had done to herself leading up to that day was much, much worse.

In high school, they shared a few classes, and in their senior year, her dream of getting closer to him had come true. She was ecstatic when they became lab partners in biology and then study buddies in English.

Once Jed hired him to work at the ranch, she was

thrilled for the chance to see more of him—whether he knew she was watching or not.

Evidently, he did know. One Friday night after he had collected his paycheck from Jed, he asked her to go for a ride in his truck. She said yes, proud to have the world—or, at least, the folks in *their* world—finally see them as a couple, too.

Only no one had seen them together at all.

They had gone for a long ride before parking near the school baseball field, where they sat and talked for hours. She was puzzled when he took her straight back to the ranch afterward. But on Saturday, she was pleased again when he finished up work and asked her out for another ride. This time, they trusted each other with glimpses into their pasts. She shared stories with him she had never told anyone else.

Yet, again, he took her directly home. Alone in her bedroom, she struggled to push away the rising doubts that kept her from falling asleep.

On Sunday night when they had driven away from the ranch in his pickup truck again, she ignored the replays of childhood memories, pushed away the nagging thoughts of the boy he had been because she saw the boy he was now. The boy who seemed proud to have her with him, too, who treated her as if she were the only girl in his world.

The boy who was giving her this magical weekend.

On Sunday, they had done very little talking...

"You can't forget what he did," Ally said.

"No, I'll never forget. And luckily, you're the only one who ever knew." Cole's attentions hadn't lasted long enough for anyone else to realize they had so briefly become partners of another kind outside English class and the biology lab.

"Why is he here, anyhow?" Ally asked.

"He didn't say."

"I'm guessing he's come back to help Layne," Ally said thoughtfully. "I heard things haven't been going too well for her. So, everything's okay—Cole will be busy with her and Scott, and you'll stay on the ranch. You'll never have to see him again."

"No, everything's not okay." She repeated what Cole had told her, which brought Ally to a halt. "Keep moving," Tina said over her shoulder. "You know I'm tracking our time." From behind her, she heard a huge sigh. Despite her tension, she couldn't hold back a smile.

Once Ally caught up to her again, she said, "He'll be working *on the ranch*?"

"Yes."

"Then, we need to find out what's going on." Ally took her by the elbow again and marched her down the street. "Let's stop in at SugarPie's and talk to Layne."

Tina kept walking but pulled her arm free. "I don't think that's a good idea. She'll just tell Cole."

"Not if we handle this right."

They were within a hundred yards of the bakery and sandwich shop when Ally came to a stop again. "That day in the cafeteria…"

"Yes," Tina said with a sigh. "That day…"

At lunch in the school cafeteria that Monday, she had invited him to the upcoming Sadie Hawkins dance. He had turned her down, then walked away—with his arm around another girl.

The rejection, coming after what he had done to her—done *with* her—the night before had left her stunned.

Yet, as much as it had hurt at the time, she had later thanked heaven for Cole's brutal response. It had made her face the reality she hadn't been able to admit during the weekend. The reality that all the magic she had seen in him was nothing but a much-practiced act full of smoke and mirrors.

Ally shook her head. "It took you forever to work up the courage to ask Cole out, didn't it?"

She nodded.

"But," Ally said softly, "if I were in your place now, I know what you'd say to me. You're not that scared high-school girl anymore, are you?"

"No, I'm certainly not." Over the past few years, she'd grown up and developed a backbone. She'd learned to stand up for herself, to be a good role model for Robbie.

Something his father could never be.

"All right, then," Ally said, "let's go inside. We can take care of two birds with one sticky bun—find out from Layne what's going on with her and get her to tell us how long Cole's staying in town." She raised her eyebrows in question.

Tina nodded firmly.

Though she had spent five years dreading the thought of seeing Cole again, she had never actually prepared for the reality.

He would be starting work on the ranch in just a few days and that didn't give her much time. Before then, she needed to find out whatever she could about his plans.

TINA AND ALLY walked through the unoccupied bakery and entered the adjoining room. The homey, country-kitchen atmosphere of the sandwich shop encouraged lingering over a cup of tea. People said the owner had planned it that way because, as a result, she heard all the gossip that traveled around Cowboy Creek.

As teens, Tina and Ally had felt sure the many small round tables in the shop were bugged.

At this time of the evening, they had their pick of the room and seated themselves at a table for two.

Tina took a deep breath, inhaling the aroma of cinnamon and cloves that always seemed to hang over the bakery and the shop. The smells here were almost as good as those in Abuela's domain at the Hitching Post.

"I don't see Layne," Ally said over the top of her menu.

"Maybe she's in the kitchen getting an order."

"I don't know... Wait—Sugar's headed this way. You know what that probably means."

Tina nodded. "She's filling in."

The owner began her day in the bakery long before the sun came up, yet could often be found in the shop at closing time. Normally, she let the waitresses handle the customers.

The wooden floorboards creaked as Sugar approached their table.

A hefty Georgia peach in her midsixties, Sugar had the softest drawl Tina had ever heard. She also had the most solid arms Tina had ever seen on anyone, including any wrangler who had ever worked on Garland Ranch. Sugar claimed she'd earned those muscles from years of kneading bread dough and hauling restaurant-sized sacks of flour.

"Hey, girls, you're in late."

"And you're working overtime," Tina said.

"Yep. Layne took the day off, so here I am."

"Darn." Ally set down her menu, giving Tina a look that said she would handle the questioning—which was fine with Tina. The less interest she showed, the less suspicion Sugar would direct her way. "We wanted to talk with her."

"Well, she'll be in tomorrow. Or you can catch her at home tonight."

"Is she spending the day with Cole? I heard he's in town."

"He is." Sugar's gray eyebrows rose as her eyes widened. "And you could have knocked me over with a sheet of parchment paper when I heard about him coming home. Layne was pretty closemouthed about it till last week." She sounded upset that she hadn't known sooner about Cole's return.

"But why is he back?" Ally asked. "I mean, he hasn't come home since he graduated high school."

"Because the ink's barely dried on Layne's divorce papers, and that rat Terry's kicking her out of the house."

Ally gasped. "But she's got Scott—and she's pregnant!"

Tina winced, thinking of the loving support she had received from Abuela and Jed all through her life, even during her pregnancy. Even though she had never told them who had fathered her child.

"Layne's situation doesn't seem to be bothering Terry," Sugar continued. "So, she called Cole."

"That's a first," Ally said, exchanging a glance with Tina. "How long is he staying?"

Ally had spoken too quickly. Sugar frowned. Resting her hands on the edge of the table, she stared from Ally to Tina and back again. "Why? What's happening?"

She didn't ask only out of curiosity. Everyone knew how well Sugar looked out for all the residents of Cowboy Creek, especially her employees.

Just the way Jed looks out for us, as Abuela would often say.

"There's nothing's happening," Tina said. But there soon would be, unfortunately.

"Yeah." Ally nodded. "I was just wondering whether I'd get to say hi or not."

"You should. Layne tells me he'll be around for a while."

Sugar chuckled. "I think coming back home again might give that boy a lot more than he bargained for."

This time, neither Tina nor Ally had anything to say.

IN HIS SISTER'S new apartment, Cole picked up one of the packing boxes he'd piled in the corner of the room. She had given the larger of the two bedrooms to her son—and his toys—and left this closet-sized one for herself.

"Scott's probably getting hungry," Layne said. "I need to start thinking about supper."

"Supper? You just gave him a three-course snack."

She laughed. "That was hours ago, Cole. And little boys have big appetites. Don't you remember from when you were a kid?"

"Not really." What he recalled was being four years old and stockpiling his own snacks, holding them aside until Layne started whining about being hungry. The sooner he could get his little sister quieted, the less chance there was of their dad yelling and sending her into tears.

As if she had read his mind, she abruptly grabbed a pile of clothes from the carton he'd set next to the closet door. "Once I have this box emptied, I'll start supper."

"We could go out," he suggested. "Or pick up some takeout. My treat, either way."

"No. The sooner I get used to cooking in that tiny kitchen, the better."

She turned to the closet. Shaking his head, he took a seat on the edge of the twin bed. He should have known she'd refuse the offer. It had been enough of a struggle getting her to agree to let him pay for some of the groceries.

She hadn't had the money to rent a truck for the move, either, and wouldn't let him get one, though he'd told her he could easily afford to pick up the tab.

In the years he'd been gone from Cowboy Creek, he had worked as a wrangler on one ranch after another.

On the run, Jed had said.

He'd rather think of it as staying open to possibilities.

In any case, he had never tied himself to anything permanent, never owned a home or even paid rent or electricity, and he had always traveled light enough to fit all his belongings into a couple of duffel bags. No sense buying things that would only weigh him down. Cheap, some folks might say, but again he preferred to look at things his way and call it being frugal.

That frugality had paid off. So had his time on the rodeo circuit. He now had a good-sized nest egg he'd been sitting on, thinking of investing.

As he'd said to Layne, what better investment could he come up with than spending some of it on his sister and her son?

He knew the answer to that question, all right. So did Layne. He would do anything for the little sister he'd raised practically single-handed.

In the years he had been gone from Cowboy Creek, he made sure to send money when she asked to borrow it, and even when she hadn't.

Deep down, he knew money could never make up for not being here for her the last few years. True, he hadn't known how bad things were between her and Terry until the end. But maybe if he'd stayed, he could have helped her out more. Been there to keep an eye on her son once in a while, so she and her now-second ex could have had some time together. Maybe that would have saved the relationship—not that he'd believed it had ever really had a chance. Neither he nor Layne knew what a good marriage looked like.

But if nothing else, helping her back then might have him feeling less like a stranger with his own sister's child now.

In the long run, his offer to get the truck for her move had done no good.

You're taking care of enough already, Layne had said.

So he had loaded his pickup and made one trip after another between her former two-story house and this so-called two-bedroom apartment.

He thought of the trip he'd made out to Garland Ranch that afternoon.

Though he and Tina had been a couple of grades ahead of Layne in school, the two knew each other. Suddenly, he felt the urge to tell Layne about running into Tina again. About what a jerk he'd been to her in high school and about how that could come back to bite him. About how he wished he'd done some things…maybe a whole lot of things…in his life differently.

But he'd never dropped his problems on his sister before and sure wouldn't start now. Not when she had enough troubles of her own.

She turned from the closet. "I talked to Sugar about giving me more time at the shop and maybe even letting me back her up when she needs help in the bakery."

"Do you really need to take on more hours, especially when it means being on your feet, in your condition? If that bast—"

"*Don't.* Please." She shot a glance toward the door. "I don't want to talk about Terry around Scott. And I can't blame Terry. If he were Scott's father, things might be different, but I can't expect the man to give me extra support for a child that's not his."

"Is he still planning to see Scott?"

"He said he would." But she wouldn't meet his eyes.

Damn. A man didn't just walk away from a child he'd raised, even if that child wasn't his own.

But he didn't push the issue. This was the first time he and Layne had discussed the subject, and he realized the wisdom of keeping the rest of his feelings about it to himself. For now.

"What about financial support for the baby?" he asked.

She touched her stomach, not much rounder than it had been the last time he'd seen her.

Late December. She had just discovered she was pregnant and hadn't wanted to be home for the holidays. They had met halfway between Cowboy Creek and the Texas ranch he was working.

For the first time since he'd left town, they had spent Christmas together. They ate dinner in a nearly empty diner decorated with limp tinsel and faded ornaments. But the waitress wore a pin with a reindeer whose nose flashed like a small red strobe light and had made Scott laugh.

Layne, expecting a baby but already on the road to divorce, had done her best to smile.

The effort it took told him he needed to come back to Cowboy Creek.

Layne shifted one of the boxes he'd set on the bed. "My lawyer's making sure Terry's keeping up with the insurance payments to cover the hospital."

"He'd damned well better keep up. You have any problems, you let me know and I'll talk to him."

"Always the protective big brother," she murmured, her eyes misting. She sat beside him and rested her head against his shoulder. "I really appreciate everything you're doing, Cole. Coming back to town. Helping with the move. Even giving me a hand with the unpacking." She sat back and looked up at him. "I couldn't have done all this without you."

"I'm not begrudging any of it, you know that. But you also have to know you're not alone here. You heard what Sugar told you the other day. You've got friends in town, plenty of friends who would help out."

"Yes, I do." She gave him a crooked smile. "Maybe I should have said what I was really thinking. I didn't *want* to do this without you."

To his dismay, her voice broke. "Layne..."

"Let me go check on Scott." She hurried from the room.

Earlier, after giving her son strict instructions to stay on the floor with his trains, she had settled him in the living room. With boxes piled throughout the apartment, it wasn't safe to let him run loose.

Cole looked at the boxes piled around him in the small bedroom and had a sudden urge to run loose himself. Or just to run. Maybe Jed hadn't been wrong, at that.

He felt the need to get the hell out of Cowboy Creek again. Coming back here had dredged up too many bad memories, too many thoughts of how helpless he'd been to protect Layne against their mama's indifference and their dad's vicious tongue.

Too many reminders of the boy he'd once been.

On the other hand, his return to help Layne through a bad time had brought with it an unexpected advantage. Taking a job at Garland Ranch again would go a long way toward proving he had changed.

His talk with Tina should have done the same, but her acceptance of his apology had rung about as true as a forced smile at a sad Christmas dinner.

He'd have to try harder to convince her they could put their past behind them.

Chapter Three

"What do you think, Paz?" Jed asked.

At the table in the hotel kitchen after breakfast, he sat finishing up his coffee. Paz stood at the counter where she was making one of her fancy desserts for tonight's supper. With Tina and Robbie at the breakfast table, they hadn't had a moment to themselves till now.

She cracked an egg into the ceramic bowl in front of her. "I think," she said, "by asking Cole to return to work here, you have stirred up more than the sugar in your coffee."

Frowning, he looked at her. She had sounded tart and a few worry lines creased her forehead, but she gave him a faint smile.

He grinned back. "I *have* set some things in motion, haven't I? For step one, anyhow."

"Do you think everything will go as you want it to?"

"Of course. All according to plan. And once the other girls are here, we'll move on to step two."

She cracked another egg into the bowl and added a spoonful of vanilla. "Sugar called me this morning. Tina and Ally were at the shop last night."

"To see Layne?"

"Yes. And asking about Cole."

He chuckled. "What did I tell you? Nothing to worry about. Everything's falling into place." At the sound of light, familiar footsteps in the hallway, he added, "Hush. Here comes the girl now." He got up to rinse his mug at the sink.

Tina entered the room and set a tray of dishes on the counter beside him. "Thank goodness for the Women's Society and their monthly breakfast! Maria's just clearing the last couple of tables. I'll take care of loading the dishwasher for you, Abuela. I'll take that, too." She plucked the rinsed mug from Jed's hand. "And then I've got to get to my office."

"Already?" he asked.

"Yes, unfortunately. And I know the next part by heart, Abuelo." She laughed. "'You can't work all day, every day.'"

"Well, it's true. You need to relax once in a while, girl. Have some fun. You work too hard."

"Somebody has to, while you brush up on being lord of the manor. You'll want to make a good impression on Andi and Jane when they get here."

"Oh, I'll make an impression on them, all right. One of these days, I might even make you sit up and take notice, too." Smiling, he left the room.

IN HER OFFICE behind the hotel registration desk, Tina entered items into the accounting software. Working with finances normally grabbed her attention, but for the past couple of days, she'd had trouble concentrating.

Again, her thoughts flew to the cause of her distraction—her brief reunion with the man who had fathered her child.

Cole had broken her heart years ago. That was nobody's fault but her own. She was over that—and over him.

Still, his return had resurrected the old memories.

She had gotten close to him, yet he had walked away from her without looking back.

Apology or no apology, if she let him get close to Robbie, how could she believe he wouldn't walk away from their son?

She pushed the thoughts of Cole from her thoughts and envisioned her little family—Robbie, Abuela and Jed. For their sakes she needed to focus on her work. On what was important to her. And that definitely didn't include Cole.

She forced her attention back to the computer screen.

Though she made sure to double-check each entry, the numbers didn't look good. Not because she hadn't totaled them correctly, but because they didn't add up to enough.

She had just finished her entries when she heard the familiar sound of Jed's boots on the stairs. His steps grew louder as he approached the front desk in the hotel lobby.

"Tina, you in there?"

"Yes," she called. "Give me a second." She hurried to back up her file and close the program.

In the kitchen that morning, Jed had seemed more like his old self. But that couldn't make her forget the past few weeks, when every time she'd tried to talk to him about her concerns, he'd brushed her off. Maybe now, he finally wanted to discuss what he had on his mind.

The office doorway led right to the lobby's registration desk. There, Jed stood with his crossed arms on the counter and one boot planted on the brass foot rail. Tall and thin, he had neatly combed his sparse white hair and wore his usual boots, jeans and Western shirt with a string tie.

Though she often lovingly teased him about being lord of the manor, as she had done in the kitchen a while earlier, there was some truth behind her words. He now left the day-to-day working of the ranch to his manager, Pete, and his cowhands, but Jed kept tabs on everything. And he always took care to project just the right image for a man who owned both a ranch and a hotel.

"Hey, my handsome *abuelo*," she said. "What's up?"

"Not much. Just checking to see if you were in there. And where's that little guy of ours?"

Her throat tightened at the thought of her son. How would she explain her years of silence about his daddy to Abuela and Jed? She swallowed hard and forced a smile. "He's in the kitchen with Abuela."

"You and Paz get all the shopping done this morning?"

"We did. She had quite a list." Unlike their trip earlier in the week.

"We'll use everything she bought. Things are gonna be a mite busier around here soon."

"You mean with Jane and Andi coming to visit?"

"That. And more." His grin made her heart fill with love—and additional concern. The low number of reservations continued to bother her. For years now, they hadn't opened the small wedding chapel on the property or even catered a reception. They would manage, especially with the bookings she had taken for later this week and the next. But they had nothing on tap for the next few months to justify Jed's level of excitement.

"Did you book a large group while we were gone?" she asked.

"Nope."

"Did half of Cowboy Creek call to reserve tables for dinner?"

He shook his head.

"Then, what? Come on, tell me."

"It's a surprise."

"Oh, really? And is this surprise the reason you've been so quiet lately?"

"Might be." He winked. "No more questions. You'll see soon enough. And I'm off to see your gran."

Relieved to have him acting like himself again, she returned to her office with a smile.

Before she could take her seat, she heard a discreet buzz, the signal Jed had set up in the hotel's office and kitchen to announce the opening of the front door. Again, she went out to the registration desk. This time, she froze behind it.

Cole Slater stood in the entryway, looking back at her.

His nephew, Scott, gave a little cry. He had seen the collection of horse figurines in the sitting room off the lobby. As if he visited the Hitching Post on a regular basis, the boy headed right toward the next room. She watched him go.

Better to focus on Scott than to stare at the man standing across the room from her. But even that didn't help, when she knew the little boy she watched was just a few months younger than her own son.

"Looks like he made himself at home," Cole said. He glanced around. "As I told Jed, this place never changes."

"Like some people I know." A pile of brochures sat on one side of the desk, the paper edges neatly aligned. She reached out to straighten them, anyhow.

"I wouldn't make snap judgments," he said.

"I don't. As you might remember from school, I'm the one who analyzes everything."

"Yeah, I do recall that."

When he approached the counter, she hid her dismay behind a frozen smile. Any second now, Robbie might come down the hall.

The minute she had seen Cole in the lobby, she had thought of what Jed had said. Her *abuelo* had been on edge for weeks, but Cole's arrival couldn't be the surprise he had referred to.

She couldn't forget what Cole had told her the other day. Jed had invited him to the ranch and then hired him again. It was odd Jed hadn't said a word about that to her beforehand. As the bookkeeper, she should have been told about a new hire. Maybe he had intended to spring Cole's return on her, after all.

Unfortunately, his secret would pale by comparison once he learned about hers.

She couldn't let the impending disaster make her forget her obligations—no matter how eagerly she wanted to run to the kitchen, grab Robbie and head for the hills. She took a deep breath and said, "Welcome back to the Hitching Post."

"Thanks. Are you managing the place now?"

"I'm the assistant manager. And bookkeeper for both the Hitching Post and the ranch."

"Bookkeeper, huh? That fits. You always were good at math."

"What can we do for you? I know you can't be looking for a room."

"Why not?"

Her fingers tightened, crumpling the long-forgotten brochure she still held. "You're staying with Layne at her new apartment, aren't you?"

"How did you know that?"

"It's a small town."

"Yeah." For a moment, he looked irritated. "And speaking of small, that describes Layne's couch. Now you mention it, the idea of taking a room here doesn't sound bad at all. It would get me off the hook for minding Scott, too." He laughed and shook his head. "And before you take me too seriously, I'm just kidding about that. But let me tell you, babysitting is not the gig for me. When I swore off marriage and kids, I should have added extended family to the list."

The statement hit her like a fist to the chest. "You don't mean that. And you wouldn't say it if you'd never had a sister or brother." *Or if you already had a child.*

Would learning about Robbie make any difference?

"In any case," he said, "I'm not looking for a room. Jed wanted me to stop by to fill out some forms."

"Why? New hires usually do that on their first day of work."

He shrugged. "Beats me. He wanted me to come by. Since I had some time as well as the kid on my hands, I thought I'd take care of it today. Is that a problem?"

"Not at all." With the rate of turnover of temporary wranglers, she always kept a blank set of employment forms on a clipboard in Jed's credenza.

"You know where Jed is?"

"In his den."

"I'll just head down there, then. Keep an eye on Scott for me, will you?"

She nodded, willing to do anything to get some space from him.

Leaving the crumpled brochure on the desk, she crossed to the sitting room and smiled at Scott. He ducked his head shyly.

Sighing, she watched him play with Robbie's favorite toys.

And she thought about Robbie's daddy.

No matter how she felt about Cole, she had to tell him the truth. What he did once he heard the news would be up to him. She had no doubts about what she had to do. Her job was to protect Robbie.

She also had to tell Abuela and Jed. They loved her

son, had helped her raise him from the moment he was born. She owed them so much, and she wanted them to hear the news first.

BY THE TIME Cole returned to the lobby, Tina stood behind the registration desk again, waiting. "All done?" she asked.

"Yep."

"Good. Now you've taken care of your business with Jed, I'm sure you'll want to head back to town. It's getting late, and Scott's hungry. He said you're all going out to dinner tonight."

"That's right."

"Scott," she called. "Your uncle's ready to go." Turning to Cole again, she added, "I've got to go help Abuela in the kitchen."

Almost sighing with relief, she began to move from behind the desk. The sound of sneakers slapping on the hallway floor froze her in place again.

"Mama?" Robbie entered the lobby and ran up to the desk. "I didn't know where you was. *Hey!*" His blue eyes widened. He pointed across the reception area at Scott, who now stood in the doorway of the sitting room cradling a toy Appaloosa. "That's *mine.*"

She couldn't manage to force a word past her tight throat.

"It's okay," Cole said, sounding as though he had trouble speaking, too. "He's not doing your horse any harm."

She kept her gaze fastened on her son. Robbie stared up at Cole, then looked toward her. After a deep breath, she said quickly, "That's right, Robbie. Scott's just playing with the horse, the way all the kids who come here do."

"He's 'sposed to keep the ponies in *there.*" He pointed toward the sitting room. "That's the rules."

"He doesn't know that," Cole said. "Why don't you and

Scott go in there with the horses? You can explain the rules to him...while your mama explains a few things to me."

"Okay." Robbie headed toward the younger boy.

Tina reached for the crumpled brochure and began smoothing it on the desktop. She could feel Cole's angry gaze on her, could feel the rush of her own anger and confusion spreading through her. Again, she fought an overwhelming desire to hurry over to Robbie, grab him by the hand and flee the hotel.

Running wasn't the answer—not that she would choose that way out, anyhow. Neither was this light-headed, weak-kneed, schoolgirl-with-a-crush reaction. She squared her shoulders. If the time had come to tell Cole the truth, to make the explanations she'd spent five long years dreading, she'd stand straight and tall and look him in the eye.

And if it came down to a battle between them, she would give him the fight of her life—and Robbie's.

For what seemed like forever, Cole stood staring at the boys in the sitting room.

Then he turned back to the desk, placed his palms flat on its surface and glared at her. "When were you planning on telling me?"

"About what?"

"About you-damned-well-know what." To his credit, he kept his voice low and even. Unfortunately, he also leaned in closer, probably to make sure she wouldn't miss a single word. "You didn't think I'd take one look at that kid and make the connection?"

"*That kid* is my son," she snapped.

"Mine, too, judging by the looks of him. He's about a year older than Scott, isn't he? Which means he's four."

The accuracy of his guess made her flinch.

"I knew it." Though he gave her a smug smile, his face

had paled. "You might've always been the math whiz in school, Tina, but I can danged sure add—"

"Stop," she whispered.

Jed was approaching from the direction of his den.

Cole shot a look over his shoulder, then turned back to her. "We're not finished," he said harshly.

"You still here?" Jed asked. "Thought you'd be long gone by now."

Cole pushed himself away from the desk. "On our way. Tina was just planning to walk us out to my truck so we could finish our conversation."

"Fine," Jed said, smiling.

"No," she blurted. "I mean...I told Cole, I've got to go help Abuela in the kitchen."

"Don't worry about that," Jed said. "Maria's in there. They've got everything covered. But I'll head on back and tell them you'll be there in a bit. Robbie, you come along with me."

She wanted to protest, but one look at Cole's narrowed eyes and set jaw told her he wouldn't leave the hotel without her—and if she refused to go, he would blurt out the truth right here.

Outside, Cole squinted against the blinding sun hovering at eye level. The strong rays showed up every faded patch of paint on his road-worn truck.

"I'm over there." He gestured to the lone vehicle.

"Come on, Scott," she said. "Let's get you into your seat so you can go and have your dinner."

As they walked ahead of him, the sun highlighted the silky length of dark braid hanging almost to Tina's waist. He'd always wanted to unravel that braid and run his fingers through her hair. She hadn't allowed him that pleasure the one time they'd been together...

He ran his hand over his face, wanting to wipe away the memory. She wasn't the only one to blame for what had happened that night. Or the only one responsible for what had come of it.

Why hadn't she said something years ago?

At the truck, while Tina strapped his nephew into place, he turned away to plant his butt against the side of the pickup. He tugged his battered hat down, blocking the sun from his eyes.

He didn't want that glare to keep him from getting a good look at Tina's face while they talked. Didn't want her finding a way to hide anything from him.

Anything else from him.

Irritation and resentment roiled inside, tightening his chest.

He looked over his shoulder. Tina must have caught the movement through the cab window. She looked up and stared right at him, her mouth closed in a firm, straight line, as if telling him she didn't plan to say a word.

No problem. He had enough words for them both.

He turned his back on her again and crossed his arms over his chest. He wasn't going anywhere until he'd said what he had to say. Yet he couldn't deny he had some pressing questions for her. For himself, too.

Most important, how was he going to handle this news that had finally sunk in, leaving him ready to keel over from the shock?

He had a son.

Memories slammed into him, bombarding him with parts of his past he'd thought long forgotten. Scenes from the rare occasions his dad bothered to notice he was alive. Times his dad would hurl nothing but scathing words his way...

You're a disgrace as a son.

You're no good.
You're worthless.

He'd never bothered to dispute anything his father said. Fighting back would only make things worse for him. Or make his dad turn his anger on Layne.

For most of his life, he had struggled not to believe anything his old man had thrown at him. But one thing was true.

With a role model like that, he didn't have a chance in hell of being a good dad.

Yet, he now had a son.

Chapter Four

Tina paused near the hood of Cole's truck and took a deep breath, trying to prepare herself for a conversation she didn't want to have.

She walked around the truck and had barely come to a stop in front of Cole before he exploded.

"Does everyone in Cowboy Creek know what you never took the trouble to tell me?"

She forced herself not to recoil from the venom in his tone. "*No.* Nobody—" Thinking of the confidences she had always shared with her best friend, she choked off her automatic response.

"And what have you told your boy? *My* boy?"

"Don't call him that." Her heart thudded at his easy assumption. "Robbie's *my* son."

"And mine. But we covered that already. Let's move on to something new. Why didn't you contact me? You must have known you were pregnant before I left town. Hell, you probably knew before graduation."

"What if I did? Why would I think you'd want to hear the result of our one-night stand?"

Her breath caught in her throat at what she had just inadvertently called her son.

She couldn't let Cole reduce her to this.

All her life, she'd been the straitlaced, logical, rational

Tina that Ally always teasingly encouraged to loosen up. All her life, except one time with Cole. A time she could never regret, since it had given her the greatest gift she had ever received.

But she needed to rely on the logical, rational Tina now. She couldn't let her emotions get in the way. She had to protect her son.

The reminder allowed her to breathe deeply and evenly again. It helped her to stay calm. "After our weekend together, you made it clear you weren't interested in me. Why would you care that I was going to have a baby?"

"Because it wasn't just yours." The muscles in his neck tightened as he swallowed hard. "Did you ever plan to tell me?"

His question vibrated with restrained emotion. The lines around his eyes deepened as if it had hurt him to ask the question. As if he were bracing himself for her reply.

An unwanted burst of compassion filled her.

She forced herself to look away and harden her heart. Where was his compassion when she'd needed it?

She glanced into the truck's rear seat. Scott sat flipping the pages of a coloring book. "If you had stayed in town," she murmured, measuring her words, "there might have been a chance you'd have found out then."

He laughed harshly. "You're in the wrong profession, Tina. You should've become a politician—except you'd have to practice maintaining eye contact. All right. Forget the double-talk. Forget I even asked. The point is, I know now. And you can just keep the news to yourself."

"I need to tell my grandparents."

"But nobody else." He shifted his Stetson and ran his hand through his hair, then stared off into the distance. "I'll need some time before we start telling other folks."

"I didn't plan to tell anyone else."

"Yeah, that's obvious," he said, his tone cold. "But I sure do." When she gasped, he narrowed his eyes. "What? Did you think I'd just walk away from this?"

This.

Forget watching what she said. Forget compassion. Now his words, tossed out so offhandedly, struck at her deepest fear.

"This *what*?" she demanded. "This confrontation? This situation? This child that's my life—not yours? I'll tell you the truth, flat-out straight, as Jed would say. Yes, I thought you would walk away. That's always been your style, hasn't it? And I want you to go. There's no reason for you to come back."

"Except that I've got a job here. And," he added, his voice dangerously soft, "now I've got other obligations."

A chill ran through her. She wrapped her arms around her middle. "You have no obligations. Not as far as I'm concerned."

"And the boy?" he said. "What about where he's concerned?"

"I'll take care of Robbie."

Yet, how could she do that completely on her own?

She had spent so much of her life with unanswered questions about her own parents…why they didn't want her, why they didn't love her, why they had left her behind for Abuela to raise.

Eventually, Robbie would have questions about his daddy, too. Questions only Cole could answer.

As if he sensed her uncertainty, as if he wanted to take advantage of her—again—he said flatly, "I couldn't have fulfilled my obligations in the past, since I never knew about the child. But now I do, I've got a lot of time to make up for."

"I won't let you—"

"'Let?'" He shoved his hat back on his head and leaned so close she could almost count each and every dark lash rimming his eyes. "You're not letting me do anything. And I'm not waiting for you to give your permission. Considering your track record, who knows how long that might take." His voice was low, deepened by emotion again. "I'm going to get to know my son."

On his first day of work, Cole parked outside the corral and walked toward Jed's barn. He couldn't keep from looking over toward the hotel. Not that he expected to see… anyone. At this early hour, the sun had barely begun to rise.

What he did see was a lighted window in the kitchen, where Paz was mostly likely getting things in order for her day. Jed and everyone else in the place ought to be sleeping.

He found the barn almost empty. Of humans, anyhow. The stalls were filled to capacity, as they always had been. Jed kept enough stock on hand to accommodate all his men and a hotel full of guests.

Half-inside one of the stalls, with his back to him, stood a man holding a shovel.

Cole paused in the doorway. Five years earlier, when he'd left the ranch without giving notice to Jed, he had walked away from Pete Brannigan and the other wranglers, too. No telling how any of them would take the news of his return to work here.

But when the man turned, Cole saw only a smile. He nodded at Pete. "Don't tell me Jed makes his ranch manager muck out stalls."

"Hey, Cole." Pete set the shovel aside and crossed the space between them to offer his hand. "He told me you were back in town and starting work today."

"That must've come as a surprise."

"What? Jed hiring someone on and telling me after the fact? No surprise there. He might call himself retired, but he's still got a strong hand on the reins."

"Always did have."

"True. Hang on a minute." Pete went into the small room partitioned off as an office and returned with a hammer and an old tin can filled with nails. "There's a pair of gloves on the workbench in the tack room. Go grab 'em." As they made their way outside, he added, "We've got some rails out by the corral that need patching. It'll get you limbered up for this afternoon. I'll be sending you out to the south border to check on the stock. You'll need to take a look at the fencing there, too."

"Trouble?"

Pete shook his head. "Just maintenance and some overly adventurous cattle. You know the drill."

At the corral, Cole wrestled a split and warped rail into submission while Pete hammered it into place.

"As for Jed and his tight rein," Pete said, "I wouldn't have it any other way. He might be past seventy, but he's still sharper than a tack. In case you were wondering."

"Should I be?"

Pete shrugged. "No idea. Just throwing that out there for old time's sake." They moved on to the next rail. "Now, your return to town, that did come as a surprise. I always figured you for having itchy feet. But maybe you scratched them enough."

"Maybe." Just the thought of tying himself down permanently in Cowboy Creek made him want to head out of town.

On feet that weren't itchy, only damned cold.

Pete swung the hammer a final time, sending the nail into place. "Let's head in, and I'll take you through the barn. Jed wants you working the corral, giving lessons to the guests as needed."

"Then I'll have to get familiar with everything you've got."

Pete nodded. "You can pick out a mount for today's ride, and another for tomorrow. You'll see a few familiar faces. But even with the new stock, we don't have anything you can't handle."

Cole followed him back toward the barn.

Jed had told him the ranch manager had a couple of kids of his own. Lucky for Pete, he'd found out about his kids at the usual time—before they were born.

He wondered how the man would deal with a situation like one he was facing. A situation he'd already managed to mess up. Yeah, he'd stood his ground with Tina. Had argued over his right to spend time with his son. Had talked the talk...

And then when the time had come to walk the walk, he'd gotten those cold feet. He hadn't come near the ranch since the night of their conversation.

No matter how much he might wish otherwise, this change in his life wasn't something he knew how to handle. Hell, he understood horses more than he did kids.

What if he couldn't be the daddy his son deserved?

IN THE HOTEL'S roomy kitchen on Sunday morning, Tina ironed the load of cloth napkins she had just removed from the dryer. She had kept herself as busy as possible for the past few days...to keep from thinking of Cole.

He had started work on the ranch, as scheduled, and she had spent those long days waiting for him to reappear at the hotel. He hadn't. Whether that meant she should thank her good fortune or worry about what revenge he was plotting, she didn't know. Either way, the uncertainty had left her barely able to close her eyes the night before.

It didn't surprise her a bit that his interest in her son hadn't lasted very long. Neither had his interest in her, years ago. She was grateful in both cases.

Seeing him again had made her recall the girl she'd once been, the girl who'd forever had the bad luck to have a crush on him. The girl who'd once wanted a family with him.

They'd *had* a child together, though Cole hadn't known that.

Till now.

Neither had anyone else.

Of course, everyone in Cowboy Creek knew four-year-old Robbie. She could just imagine their well-meaning but frantic conversations when they had found out she was pregnant.

Do you think the daddy's one of Jed's full-time ranch hands?

Or a wrangler who worked there only for a season?

Maybe he was a guest who stayed at the Hitching Post and never came back again.

She didn't know what conclusions they had come to. After telling Ally the truth, she had left everyone else to speculate all they wanted—and hoped they would never stumble upon the truth. Soon, thanks to Cole, they would never have to guess again.

She regretted only that she had never told her grandparents. But now the time was coming for her to let them know the truth about Robbie—and Cole—she wasn't sure she would ever find the right words.

"I'm glad we had a few people in the dining room this morning," Abuela said.

Happy for the distraction from her worries, Tina nodded. Luckily, they usually did get a small crowd for their Sunday brunch. Today had been no exception, although the dining room had cleared out now.

Things were looking up for the hotel, as well. A young couple had checked in the night before, and two other parties had booked rooms for the coming week.

They would fill a couple of rooms with family, too. Her cousin Jane had already arrived, and Andi and her children were due in from the airport at any time.

With so many people around, Tina hadn't found the chance to talk to her grandparents alone.

"Of course, you're glad to have guests in the dining room, Abuela. You're always happier when we have more mouths to feed."

"That's what I do," Abuela said simply. "But I'm sorry you had to take Maria's place."

The waitress who usually worked the morning shift on the weekend attended classes part-time at the community college. In a panic, Maria had taken the day off to study for an upcoming midterm exam.

"Maria is a good girl," Abuela said, "but when it comes to her schoolwork, she's not very organized at all. I'm so happy you were always dependable, never waiting till the last minute to study for your tests."

Tina stared down at the napkin she was pressing.

Yes, she was dependable and reliable. As Jed often said, she was as steady as they made them—which meant her one slip had always been so much harder to explain.

"Filling in around here is what *I* do," she said lightly. Waitress, maid, ranch hand for some of the dude ranch activities—she'd done all those jobs and more. Running a family-owned business meant pitching in whenever you were shorthanded. "I'm just glad I never had to fill in for *you.* I'll never be the cook you are, no matter how many lessons you give me."

"That's not a bit true. You are an excellent cook. And someday you will be an excellent wife."

Tina flinched. Quickly, she covered her reaction by grabbing a few more napkins from the basket.

Abuela couldn't know how much those words had hurt.

She loved both her grandparents and knew how much they loved her. Unlike her parents, they had always been there for her.

For a while after learning her parents had abandoned her, she had felt lost and alone, except with Abuela and Jed and at her home here at the Hitching Post. The attic room upstairs became her sanctuary. The hotel she loved, with its hundred years of history, became her connection to the past. And her dreams of the future were filled with images of the family she had with Cole.

A SHORT WHILE LATER, hearing Jed's footsteps approaching the kitchen, Tina managed a smile.

He entered the room grinning. "We've got a couple more guests in for brunch. Cole and his sister's boy."

His words startled her, but she fought to behave naturally.

She unplugged the iron and went to return it to the shelf in the walk-in pantry. Over her shoulder, she said, "The dining room's closed."

"Not for old friends, it isn't. Go see what he wants to eat, will you?"

Like it or not—and she didn't—she had to face Cole.

On her way out of the room, she picked up an order pad from the china cabinet near the kitchen door. She forced herself to walk down the hall and through the reception area.

From the dining room, she heard Cole's deep voice followed by her cousin's husky laugh.

At the doorway, she stopped. In the otherwise vacant room, Cole and Jane were seated at a table for four near a sunlit window, and Robbie and Scott knelt on chairs at a large table in one corner of the room.

Delaying the inevitable, she focused on that corner table. To her dismay, the boys had already pushed aside the cutlery and lined up a row of plastic farm animals on the tabletop between them. She would have a hard time tearing Robbie away from his play.

She could understand her son's interest in Cole's nephew. Other than an occasional guest at the hotel, Robbie was almost as cut off from companionship his own age here at the ranch as she had been as a child. The ranch manager had a couple of kids, but as far as Robbie was concerned, Pete's five-year-old daughter was "too bossy" and his two-year-old son was "no fun."

Reluctantly, she tore her gaze away from the boys and looked at Cole.

Jane spotted her standing in the doorway. "Tina," she said brightly, "where have you been? You've got a hungry man waiting here."

"Have I?"

"Yes. I hope you're ready to take his order."

In answer, Tina held up the pad.

"Then I'll turn him over to you." After smiling at Cole, Jane rose from the table. As usual, Tina's older cousin wore black from head to toe and had shoulder-length dark hair. From the chair beside the one she'd been sitting in, she lifted one of the two cameras she had brought to the ranch with her. "Think I'll go shoot some local color."

As she left the room, Tina plastered a professional smile on her face and went toward Cole's table.

In all the years since he had left Cowboy Creek, she had never let herself imagine him here at the ranch again. That would have been too poignant a reminder of the dream that would never come true.

Now that he was sitting in front of her, he was a reminder of all she needed to protect. "What are you doing here?" she demanded, keeping her voice low.

"Layne's working this morning, so I thought I'd give her a break and bring Scott over for brunch. Since I was headed here, anyway."

She didn't miss the unstated warning. He intended to make good on what he had told her the other night. He intended to see Robbie whether she wanted him to or not. She looked from the pot of coffee in front of him to his comfortably sprawled position at the table. Both told her he wouldn't be in a rush to leave.

He gestured to the empty chair across from his. "Join me?"

"I've already eaten." She clamped her hands around the order pad. She had work to do. A long list of reasons to stay away from him. A longer list of reasons to take Robbie out of this room. She had an even more pressing need to find out what Cole was up to. "Robbie is only a four-year-old," she said, speaking softly but struggling to keep her tone even. "You can't just walk in here out of nowhere and turn his life upside down."

"You really think that's what I've come to do?" He waved as if to brush the question away. "No, don't answer that. I think I already know."

"Then, what is it you've got in mind?"

"Take a seat and you'll find out."

At the end of their conversation at his truck the other day, she'd wanted only to get him off the ranch.

Now that he was here again and pushing her, she wanted to push back. But that could turn the situation into a custody battle, a fight with them on different sides and her son caught in the middle. She couldn't risk that.

After a glance at the corner table where the boys sat engrossed in noisy play, she took the seat across from Cole. "What is it you want?"

"To spend some time with my son."

"But I told you, no one here—" She cut herself off, again unwilling to finish the thought ringing inside her head.

No one here on the ranch knows you're my child's father.

Saying it aloud would make it more real—and make her feel somehow more vulnerable to any retaliation Cole might have planned.

"Yeah, I remember," he said drily. "Nobody knows. Well, Jed and Paz are the only ones who count. Once you tell them, we can work around everybody else."

He glanced toward the boys, then back at her. "There's no point in arguing," he said flatly. "I want to be a part of my son's life. And once he gets used to having me around, I intend to tell him I'm his daddy."

She flinched, still not able to handle hearing those words.

Somehow, she had half hoped he had changed his mind about Robbie, about working here, about staying in town to help his sister. When he hadn't shown up this morning, she had hoped he had left Cowboy Creek again forever.

But no, here he was, just as adamant about spending

time with Robbie as Robbie would be about having playtime with Scott.

Like father, like son.

Chapter Five

Cole finished his brunch platter in the dining room, where the only sound came from the boys playing with their toys.

He stared as Tina's son...*his* son knelt in his chair and leaned forward to slide a plastic giraffe across the table. The kid looked so young, and nearly the same size as Scott. Short for his age, like Tina had been, and with hair almost as dark as hers. Those similarities wouldn't have given him a clue that he'd fathered the child, but there was no missing the boy's eyes, so unlike Tina's bottomless dark brown ones. Eyes as blue as his own.

From the direction of the lobby, he heard voices, laughter, the sound of a door closing.

A few minutes later, Jed appeared in the wide doorway of the dining room. Jane, dressed all in black, stood on one side of him. On the other, a slim blonde woman in a brightly colored shirt and pants held a baby in one arm. Pressed next to her stood a boy who looked to be a few months younger than Scott.

Jed wrapped his arms around the women's shoulders. "Look who I've got here. Cole, of course you saw Jane just a bit ago." He hugged the dark-haired woman with the cameras. "But you might not recall meeting my other granddaughter. This is Andi and her kids." He beamed at the trio.

Cole nodded and forced a smile but said nothing. Making polite conversation wasn't high on his list right now. Much as he'd looked forward to some time this morning to reconnect with his old boss, he didn't care to sit down to a meal with the man's family. At least, not right this minute.

He hadn't simmered down yet after that conversation with Tina. Obviously, she didn't like having him around. But he wasn't going anywhere.

Jed urged the women forward. "Cole, bring your coffee over to the big table and join us."

Andi shuffled a few steps with her little boy holding her pants leg in a near-death grip.

Maybe the kid had picked up on the tension Cole could almost feel radiating from him. Not that he had anything against Jane and Andi. He remembered them both, all right, from when he'd worked for Jed. The two girls and their families had spent summer vacations and school holidays at Garland Ranch. It looked like they were continuing the tradition.

Jane had seemed relaxed enough when they'd talked earlier, but the blonde, Andi, seemed ill at ease. Or as if she had something troubling her.

Tina, who had just come back into the room, looked almost as distracted. *She* surely must have a lot on her mind.

What had she thought of his absence for the past few days, especially after the way he'd insisted on spending time with Robbie? She wouldn't have missed him, that was for sure. More likely, she probably felt relieved not to have him around.

And she must dread the thought of breaking the news to their son.

For a second, he almost felt sorry for her. But then he thought again of how she'd deceived him.

"Well, come on," Jed urged, "everyone take a seat. You girls and this little guy must be hungry after your travels.

Tina, you get them all settled in while I go tell your gran that Andi and the kids have arrived."

Jed left the room with more spring in his step than Cole would have expected from a man his age. Obviously, having his granddaughters visit had made his day.

Reluctantly, Cole grabbed his mug and the coffeepot and moved to the center table.

From the corner, Robbie called, "Mama, Scott and me are gonna go play with the ponies, okay?"

She nodded. "All right, but stay in the sitting room with them."

"I know. That's the rules."

He rushed across the room, leaving the plastic animals he'd been playing with scattered all over the tabletop. Cole had trouble holding back a smile. Naturally, any kid of his would choose horses over a handful of other animals.

Scott hotfooted after Robbie as if the pair were best buddies. As they might have been, if things had been different.

No, as they might very well be. How the hell would he know?

He swallowed another wave of resentment at Tina.

Suddenly, he thought of Layne. Had *she* known and kept quiet about Tina's pregnancy, too?

He refused to think that of his own sister.

But he wouldn't put anything past Tina.

ONCE ROBBIE AND SCOTT had left the dining room, Tina didn't know where to look. At her cousin Jane. At her other cousin Andi and her children. Or at Jed, who stood beside the table in the center of the room.

She definitely didn't want to make eye contact with Cole, who had just taken the chair next to hers.

She glanced down the length of the table, where Jed stood beaming at Andi's children. Her little boy was now almost three and her baby only a few weeks old. Neither Andi nor Jane had visited for quite a while, and though Jed seldom complained how infrequently he saw them, she knew how much he missed them all.

"Well," he said, "first, I've got to give these great-grandkids of mine a big hug."

At Jed's words, the boy hid behind his mother. Smiling, Andi reached up to place her daughter into Jed's waiting hands. The sight of him cradling his infant great-granddaughter made Tina blink back tears. It seemed like only a few short months ago he'd held Robbie the same way.

Jed took his seat, still holding the baby.

Abuela came from the kitchen with a platter of her sugary sopaipillas. She hugged Andi and exclaimed over Andi's children. Then, to Tina's surprise, she gave Cole a warm welcome and a glowing smile.

The unexpected brunch turned into a fiesta, a celebration for everyone except Tina, who struggled to ignore Cole.

"I remember you." Andi smiled at him. "You used to work for Grandpa, didn't you?"

"I did, back in high school." Though he returned the smile, Tina could hear the strain in his voice. "And as of last week, I'm back to working here again. Looks like Jed just can't get rid of me."

Neither could she.

For some reason this family gathering seemed to have made him uncomfortable, which made her think of his remark about swearing off family. Maybe he hadn't been joking about his feelings, after all. How much time had he spent with Layne and Scott, his own family, over the past few years?

He hadn't come back to town during that time, but she

knew from things Sugar had said that Layne occasionally had gone to visit him. Did she miss her brother, the way Jed missed his sons and their families?

In all these years, had Cole missed Layne and Scott?

If he left Cowboy Creek again, would he ever think about Robbie?

Tina didn't add much to the conversation flowing around her. She usually stayed quiet in crowds. But as the minutes ticked away, she forced herself to follow the comments. Anything to keep from thinking of what would happen when she and Cole left the room.

He had come here today determined to spend time with Robbie, and he would want to go look for her son.

She didn't need the narrow-eyed glances he shot at her from time to time to remind her of that. She also didn't need him hovering near her elbow as if to keep her from disappearing.

To tell the truth, she didn't need him here at all.

She felt grateful her cousins had chosen this week to come for a visit. Their conversation helped cover her silences. And without them here, Jed and Abuela would have made Cole the center of attention.

When Jed had finished his last bite of dessert, he pushed his plate away and clasped hands with Andi and Jane, who sat on either side of him.

"Now that you two have arrived," he said, "I'm not letting you go very far. And I've got some mighty important plans to share with you about this hotel."

Her breath caught. First, Jed had stunned her by rehiring Cole. And now this. What plans?

"You all have always known the Hitching Post is my pride," he continued. "The weddings were my Mary's joy, but I've let that side of things go for a long time. Not anymore. My dream is to get this place back to the way it was, with the catering business up and running."

She stared at him in astonishment. She had lived on this ranch since she'd been born, and Jed had always known how much she loved the hotel. Yet never once had he said a word to her about his dream.

"That's a wonderful idea, Grandpa," Andi said. "Weddings are a booming business. I know people who would love to have a private ceremony at a ranch setting like this."

"The hotel's got great character," Jane agreed. "You ought to capitalize on the honeymoon angle, too." She looked around, eyeing the bright glazed pottery on the table, the half-paneled walls, the ceiling crisscrossed by dark beams. "You'd have to update, make some renovations, but keep the Southwestern style."

Tina gripped her napkin with both hands. This was too much. Jed's idea for attracting guests and increasing the hotel's profits was wonderful. Lord only knew, they could use the revenue.

But...*renovations*?

They couldn't afford to do anything much except paint and buy new linens. That would be fine with her. But structurally, there wasn't a single thing about the hotel she would want to see changed.

"A 'Southwestern destination wedding,'" Jane murmured, making air quotes with one hand. Or maybe she imagined snapping a photo with one of the cameras she'd left on a side chair. Eyes narrowed, she nodded. "I can see it."

"So can I," said Jed, slapping his hand on the tabletop. "I want the Hitching Post made into a going concern again. But here's the thing. With everything that'll need to be done around this place, I can't tackle it alone. I want all you girls to turn my dreams into reality."

Tina started. She couldn't keep from feeling touched that Jed wanted her help to achieve his dreams.

But the rest of his statement left her wary. If the last thing she wanted for the hotel was to see it changed, the next-to-last thing was having to coordinate those changes with her cousins. She had long ago seen the way they played with others: they didn't.

"All of us, Grandpa?" Jane asked, as if she had her own doubts about Jed's idea.

"Yep. You're a photographer. You can pull together some photos that will put this place on the map. Tina's got the financial know-how to deal with the upgrades. And we'll get Andi helping with something, too."

Both women looked as astonished as she felt.

Between Jed's announcement and her cousins' involvement and Cole's sudden reappearance, her life had spun out of control.

AFTER SPENDING A while listening to the Garlands discuss Jed's ideas for the hotel, Cole excused himself. "I'll go join Scott and Robbie."

"Me go boys!" Andi's son shouted.

His mama looked at Cole. He hoped his nod of agreement appeared more enthusiastic than it felt. He didn't begrudge taking the little one along, but he had enough to handle just getting to know the two older boys.

"All right, Trey." Andi lifted him down from his high chair. "You be good and play nice."

The kid didn't look much younger than Scott, yet as he toddled along, he seemed uncertain on his feet. Since his nephew had been just as shaky when they'd met at the diner a few months ago for their Christmas dinner, Cole knew enough now to shorten his stride.

What he didn't know was what it would have been like

to see his own son like a newborn calf trying out his legs. Taking his first steps. And maybe tumbling a time or two until he got the hang of things.

Thanks to Tina, there were a lot of things he'd never know.

The thought made him stop in his tracks.

Beside him, Andi's son stopped, too, and tugged on Cole's jeans. "Me go?"

"Yeah," Cole said. "Don't you worry, pardner. We're going." He wasn't about to miss this chance to spend some time with Robbie, especially now he could be in a room without the boy's mama watching like a hawk.

He had seen her face when he'd stood to leave the dining room. It was clear she didn't want him with his own kid without her there to supervise.

The two boys had lined up the collection of plastic horses on the sitting room floor. Cole walked between the toys, watching where he set his heavy boots and keeping an eye out for anything in the kid's path.

They took seats on the floor, Trey crawling over to the boys and Cole leaning up against the couch. To his surprise, Jed entered the room holding Andi's daughter. "I thought you and the girls were busy making plans."

"They're talking drapes and comforters, so I left them to it. I'll be on hand when they get into the more important stuff." He took a seat in the low-slung chair near the couch. "Thought I'd keep you company for a bit."

Or had Tina sent his boss to take her hawk-eyed place?

But no need for such a crazy notion. If he could believe what she'd said—that Jed and Paz didn't know about the boy—she could hardly have asked Jed to observe him with Robbie.

Cole stretched his legs out, crossing his boots at the ankle. From this position, he could see the boys and Jed.

As he sat watching the old man with the baby cradled in his big, gnarled hands, he had to swallow another wave of resentment at Tina.

He had meant it when he'd told her there was no sense wasting any more time. Thinking of all he had missed of his son's life, he looked at Jed with his great-granddaughter and shook his head.

Obviously unaware of Cole's train of thought, Jed caught his reaction and grinned. "Nothing like it."

For a second, he felt like spilling his guts to the man. But that wouldn't help the situation. He remained silent about his newfound fatherhood and went into the role he hoped he could play. "Holding a newborn? No, thanks, I'll pass. Keeping an eye on Scott's more than enough for me."

"Not just the holding, but the having," Jed said solemnly. "Knowing a part of Mary and me lives on in this little girl, there's nothing like that feeling. Nothing like family."

Cole didn't respond.

"Got any plans for settling down yet?"

"No." *Not yet. Not ever.* He'd learned the hard way marriage wasn't in the picture for him.

"Ah, you're young. You'll change your mind."

"I doubt it."

"Then maybe some young lady will change it for you, the way my Mary did mine. Considering the handful of women we've got here in the hotel right now, you ought to find one to strike your fancy."

Cole laughed. "What are you trying to do, get your granddaughters married off?"

"Might be." The old man looked thoughtful. "I just wish—" He stared into space.

After a few moments of watching him, Cole frowned. "What are you wishing for?"

"Nothing we need to discuss."

The statement and his abrupt tone came as a surprise.

"Being hardheaded doesn't get a person very far," Jed continued. "You'll learn that sometime, sooner than later if you're lucky."

"I'm not hardheaded. I just know my mind."

"Ha." The older man sounded skeptical but didn't elaborate. He rose from his seat with the baby in one arm. "Think I'll head into the kitchen and give Paz a turn. She'll want to hold this little girl, even if you don't."

"As I told you, I've got enough to do watching Scott. Who knew a three-year-old could be such a handful."

Jed laughed. "Easy to see you weren't around much during your nephew's 'terrible twos.' Now, that's an age for you. We had quite a time of it with Robbie."

"Did you?" Another of his son's stages he had missed. "Guess you've had your hands full helping out with him since he was born."

"Me and Paz both," Jed agreed.

Cole waited, but the older man didn't add anything. He had responded naturally enough to the comment, though.

After Jed left, Cole sat watching the boys. Scott and Robbie had taken most of the horses, leaving only a couple for Andi's son, Trey. As the oldest and owner of the toys, Robbie seemed to be in charge.

"What are you doing?" Cole asked. His chest tightened, almost as if he'd held his breath. This was the first conversation he had initiated with his son.

From now on, *everything* that happened would be a first for them.

The boy eyed him without speaking, taking his time with a response. Taking *his* measure, Cole figured. Robbie didn't seem fearful or wary. Living here in the hotel, he was probably used to having lots of folks around.

Finally, he said, "We're playing horses."

"And what's that?" Cole pointed to two empty cardboard boxes standing on their sides.

"That's the corral. The ponies have to stay inside."

"Why?" Andi's son demanded.

"So they don't run away."

"Why do they run away?" Scott asked.

Robbie frowned. "I don't know." After a long pause, he turned to Cole. "Why?"

The boy looked like Tina. Even more, his solemn expression made him think of her in their high-school biology class, where she always took things so seriously. She was especially strict while overseeing experiments that, if not for her, he would probably have messed up.

He didn't want to mess up now. "Well...maybe the ponies want to find other horses to play with. Or maybe they want to break free of the corral."

"Do you think that's why they run away?" Robbie asked.

"Could be. They like to be free."

That's what he had wanted. To break free. Free from the constant tension he and Layne lived with while their dad was alive. From the sympathy of the folks—the clueless folks—in town once his dad had passed on. And, almost worst of all, from the never-ending reminders they'd hear from their mom, who just couldn't let memories of the man die with him.

"Then, no more corral." Laughing, Robbie knocked over his carefully erected pair of boxes. His wide grin again reminded Cole of Tina and the very few times he'd seen her laugh aloud.

Judging by Jed's nonresponse a few minutes ago, she must have been telling the truth when she'd said no one on the ranch knew about Robbie's daddy.

Robbie's daddy.

She sure hadn't liked him calling himself that.

She had never wanted him to know the truth.

Years ago, he would never have believed sweet Tina capable of such deception.

He had known she'd been hung up on him all through school, but when he'd started asking girls out, he hadn't looked her way. She was quiet. Reserved. And so serious about so many things he'd had no plans ever to get serious about. He still didn't.

He had liked her a lot back then. Sometimes he even dreamed about her. But he knew better than to let himself be tied down. Instead, he'd gone from girl to girl, never getting too involved, never putting his heart on the line. Until senior year.

He'd let down his guard for one weekend, had lowered his defenses long enough to trust Tina. But not long enough to trust himself.

The guards had gone up again, the defenses had been put back in place, and the next day in the cafeteria, he had turned down her invitation to the dance and walked away.

Maybe he hadn't done it nicely.

All right, yeah, he'd been an ass. A typical, teenaged-male ass.

That didn't give her the right to cheat him of all these years with his son.

Chapter Six

Once Jed had left the unexpected business meeting in the dining room, Tina's cousins did most of the talking. Her mind kept wandering to Cole and Robbie. If they were together, she wanted to be there, too.

As soon as she could, she left Jane and Andi and made her way to the lobby.

In the reception area, she saw Jed ambling down the hall toward her from the direction of the kitchen.

Cole barreled through the sitting room doorway. A quick look past him showed all three boys playing happily with Robbie's ponies. Nothing wrong there.

Yet when she met Cole's gaze, his narrowed eyes told her she wouldn't like hearing whatever he had on his mind.

Slipping into her professional role, she stepped behind the registration desk.

By the time Jed joined them, Cole had gotten his expression under control and found a smile. "You know, Jed, I've rethought the idea about staying at Layne's. Considering how early I need to report in here every day, I'll only throw off her morning routine and probably interfere with Scott's sleep schedule. I'd like to take a bed in the bunkhouse, after all."

She froze. She didn't want him living so close to the

hotel, having so much access to Robbie. When Jed shook his head, she could barely hold back her sigh of relief.

"Nope. That won't work," he said. "We haven't got a bed free in the bunkhouse right now."

She blinked in surprise. They had room for several more wranglers. Why Jed would refuse to put Cole up in the bunkhouse, she didn't know, but she felt immensely grateful.

Until he added, "But that's no problem. We've got plenty of rooms right here." He turned to her. "Tina, take care of the man, will you?"

Her heart sank. "But...we've never had a ranch hand stay in the hotel."

"Then maybe it's high time we did. You know the cowhands are one of the biggest draws on this ranch." He grinned. "Imagine folks checking in and finding a real, live cowboy joining them for their meals. They'll get a kick out of it."

"But..." She stopped.

When she made financial recommendations for the ranch or the hotel, Jed always heard her out. But naturally, as he owned the properties, the final decisions rested with him.

The look of smug satisfaction on Cole's face said he realized she had no choice.

Jed sauntered down the hall again.

She raised her chin and glared at Cole.

"Is there a problem?" He glanced around the vacant lobby. "It doesn't look like you're all booked up. In fact, from what I saw this morning and the other day, you could use some customers."

"Guests," she corrected. "And you're not serious."

"Why not?"

"You don't need to take a room."

"Oh, yes, I do. You heard what I said to Jed about messing up Layne's schedule."

"And that was a load of bull."

"No, it wasn't. Besides, remember what I told you about her short couch? A few nights sleeping on that were enough to convince me to move over here."

"You don't need to do this," she insisted, her voice strained. "I told you, you can see Robbie."

"Yeah, you did. But look at the odds. You kept my son a secret from me for all these years. You haven't even told your own grandparents the truth. How can I trust you to keep your word?"

"That's ridiculous. *I'm* the trustworthy one standing here. I'm the one who doesn't run from responsibility."

"Maybe so. But suppose you'd given me the news a long time ago. How do you know I wouldn't have stayed in town?" He leaned over the counter, pressing his point home. "As of now, I'm staying right here in this hotel. If you won't check me in, I know someone who will."

"I'm telling you, Paz, you should've seen the look on those kids' faces when I told Tina to book Cole into the hotel." Jed laughed and slapped his hand on the kitchen table.

"You were careful, I hope?"

"Well, of course, I was." He took the baby from Paz's arms. "After all, I didn't tell her to give him a room in our family wing, did I? Now, that would have been a dead giveaway." He looked down at the baby. "Your great-granddaddy's got more smarts than that, hasn't he?"

"Tina has smarts, too," Paz said.

"And plenty of them," he agreed. He shook his head. "It's not easy getting anything past that girl. She already questioned me. You'd have thought I wanted to bring a live bull into the hotel, instead of just a cowhand. But my answers satisfied her."

"And now?"

"Now we sit back for a bit and watch the fun. It won't do to rush things, or for sure Tina will think something's up. Cole, too. Although I do need to make a note to see Pete tomorrow."

Paz was already well into her menu for tonight's supper, but she looked up from her preparations. "Did you talk to Cole at all?"

"I did. After you left the dining room I tracked him to the sitting room. He tells me he doesn't want to settle down."

Her eyes widened. "You asked him that already?"

"Yep. I figured it's best for us to find out what we're up against as soon as we can. And along the way in our conversation, I planted a few seeds." He smiled down at the baby again and chucked her under her chin. "Wait and see. We'll have a bunch of little ones like you running around here in no time."

WHEN ALLY CALLED late that afternoon with an urgent request to meet after work, Tina had jumped at the chance. She needed the exercise to relieve her stress and the space from her family. Most of all, she needed to leave the hotel. Thanks to Cole, the home she had always loved suddenly seemed more like a prison. And he hadn't even moved into the Hitching Post yet.

As if she could outrun her thoughts, she picked up her pace.

It took Ally a moment to catch up. "Guess who I saw today," she said.

Thinking she meant Cole, Tina almost missed a step.

But, no, her best friend wouldn't tease her about him. "Your cute wrangler?"

Ally rolled her eyes. "I saw the wheels turning, Tina. You analyze the fun out of everything. But you're right—and he's cuter than ever."

"And by my analysis of your grin, I'd say you finally got him to look your way."

"Right again. I gave him the come-hither look, like in all those old movies my mama loves, and he couldn't resist." She batted her mascaraed lashes. "His name's Stan, he's from Dallas, and he's working at Rollins Ranch."

"Permanently?"

"For the season. Unless I can get him to change his mind."

Would Cole change his mind about some things, too, now that he knew he had a child? She wondered how long he expected to keep his room at the hotel. How long he planned to work for Jed.

How long he would stay in town.

And she couldn't help wondering whether he would make a genuine attempt to get close to Robbie.

"Hello?" Ally said.

She blinked. "Sorry. I'm just tired."

"And...?"

She sighed. "And...Cole's taking a room at the Hitching Post."

"What?"

She gave her friend an abbreviated version of what had happened over the past few days.

Ally came to a halt on the sidewalk. "*No.* Now what are you going to do?"

"I have no idea yet. But keep moving," she directed over her shoulder. She had tossed and turned all night. If she stood in one place, she might fall asleep on her feet.

"I don't see him hanging around for very long," Ally said in that uncanny way she sometimes had of reading Tina's mind. "After all, he already left once before. Why don't you just wait him out? Maybe if you don't make a big deal over him with Robbie, he'll disappear again. *If* you want him to disappear, that is... Do you?"

"I don't know." She looked down Canyon Road to the red-tinged mountains in the distance. Except for college classes and licensing exams, she'd rarely gone beyond Cowboy Creek's town limits. In the past five years, Cole hadn't ventured back over the line. No matter his situation at the moment, what were the chances he would want to live here permanently? "I have no idea what his plans are." She sighed. "Part of me hopes he'll stay for Robbie's sake. I don't want my son growing up without a daddy."

"Like you did."

"Like I did," she agreed.

And part of her hoped Cole would stay...for reasons that, as analytical as she might be, she couldn't seem to figure out. Those reasons were too hazy to explain to Ally. Too complicated even for her to think about right now.

Deliberately, she changed the subject and told Ally about the arrival of her cousins.

"Bet your *abuelo*'s happy. It's been a while. What's going on with them?"

"Jane's busy and out of the country half the time. And Andi's still with her in-laws in Scottsdale. She's had the baby, a beautiful little girl."

"Did she lose her flat stomach?"

"No. She's already back to her prepregnancy shape."

"Humph." Ally race-walked a few feet ahead, then slowed down again. "Skinny little rich brat."

"Stop, Ally. Those days are over. You can't keep calling her that just because we've got trouble watching our weight."

"*Ha.* The only thing I watch is my mama's burritos—when I'm eating them."

Tina laughed. "Sure. And too many goodies from in *there*." Ally had slowed again, this time on the sidewalk in front of SugarPie's. Tina grabbed her by the elbow and propelled her past the bakery.

"Oh, all right," Ally said. "Besides, who's got trouble? You know I like that old saying, if you've got it, flaunt it." And she always did. This afternoon, she wore a tie-dyed leotard with red micro-minishorts—and of course, her purple running shoes. "I'm sorry."

She had said the words so solemnly, Tina stared at her in confusion.

"I feel terrible about Andi losing her husband. You know I do." Ally shrugged. "But other than that, really, why are you worrying over what I say about those girls? Growing up, they wouldn't give you the time of day—even when they wore all those fancy watches you liked so much."

"One watch each, Ally. It was the fourteen necklaces and bracelets I coveted."

"Don't be such an accountant."

Ally smiled to take out the sting. Tina hadn't felt one. She was used to her friend's teasing about her job.

Yet Ally's comment had also hit a serious note.

Two years younger, Tina had always looked up to her cousins. When their families came to the ranch for vacations, Andi and Jane had brought the latest clothes, which she had no money of her own to buy back then. They'd worn makeup, which she never used. They had both been so slim, sophisticated and beautiful, Jane with her black hair against milk-white skin and Andi with a princess's blond hair and blue eyes.

They had always been closer to each other than they ever had been to her, though she was Jed's granddaughter, too... The illegitimate daughter of his son and the hotel cook's daughter. As a result, Jane and Andi had always made her feel second-best.

Jed, oblivious to all that years ago, now expected her to work with them. And she would. She had grown up and gotten over her childhood feelings, even if uncomfortable memories sometimes resurfaced.

She had experienced that more than she'd wanted to this week.

"Look," Ally said, "don't let those women get you down. They'll be gone soon, anyway, won't they?"

She nodded. "Yes. They're only staying a week or two. But they'll be back to help Jed. Eventually." She explained Jed's plans to revitalize the Hitching Post. "Meanwhile, Andi's going to talk to a few friends about wedding planners. Jane's job keeps her on the run, but when we're ready, she's going to set up a website." She took a deep breath. "And since I'm the one with the accounting degrees, I'm taking care of the first phase. Financing for the renovations."

"Renovations?"

Ally came to a halt once again. This time, Tina didn't prod her. Instead, she stopped and stared at the building beside them. The bookstore was one of her favorite places to spend time when she came to town. The store's front window currently held a display of children's classics, every one of which she knew nearly by heart. Every one of which she had planned to read to *all* of her and Cole's children.

Ally rested her hand on her shoulder and said just the

words Tina had hoped she wouldn't say. "But...the hotel... your home..."

She shrugged. "That doesn't matter."

Ally blew out an exasperated breath. "Because those girls want to get the place all fancied up."

"No, because Jed wants it that way."

"But this isn't right. I know you don't want anybody making changes to the hotel."

"That doesn't matter, either. These are Jed's dreams."

Her own dreams, the ones she hadn't been able to share even with Ally, had slipped away. She had done nothing to try to catch them. She shouldn't have wished for things that could never be hers in the first place.

She shouldn't wish for anything now.

AT LAYNE'S THAT EVENING, Cole helped unpack boxes while she put her son's clothes away in his closet. He watched her gaze go yet again to the bedside table and the clown with the clock in its stomach.

Finally unable to contain his irritation, he muttered, "I can take a run to the L-G Store and pick up a half gallon of ice cream."

Again, she looked at the clock. "Let's wait awhile. It's early yet. Terry promised he'd take Scott to the Big Dipper tonight."

"And how many promises has he broken in the boy's lifetime?"

"Plenty," she admitted. She turned back to the closet.

He opened a few more packing boxes and went back to the subject of his previous thoughts. Tina. He had decided to stay at the Hitching Post to see the child, not her. Then why couldn't he get her out of his mind?

"I don't understand," she said.

"Neither do I," he said before he could catch himself.

He looked up at Layne, who stood in the bedroom doorway looking at him, her expression puzzled. *Time to improvise.* "I don't understand how one child not even five years old yet could wind up with so many clothes."

She laughed. "As you said the other day, I have friends. But what *I* still don't understand is why you've decided to stay at the ranch."

Because he'd taken a stand with Tina, and he wouldn't back down.

And because it would put him closer to his son.

But he couldn't say either of those things to Layne.

He looked around him. "The bedrooms here are spoken for and, with all those boxes in the living room, I was finding it hard to breathe."

"Since when have you been claustrophobic?"

Since I saw Tina again.

He tried to smile.

"You're the one who insisted on sleeping there," she reminded him. "I offered you my bedroom. No, that's not your real reason... I'm wondering if Tina Sanchez has something to do with your decision."

He froze. "Why would you think that?"

"Oh, I don't know...for one thing, it seems odd that you didn't say a word about staying at the ranch until you came back from there this afternoon. And for another thing, I'm remembering when we were in high school and for a while I heard nothing but 'Tina this' and 'Tina that.'"

"Yeah. 'Tina, the slave driver.'"

She laughed. "Yes. Before that, I don't think I'd ever seen you sit down with a textbook. At first it *was* all about the homework she made you do. Then things changed, and it wasn't 'Tina, the slave driver' anymore."

"Your memory must be going. And that's not why I took the room."

Her eyes narrowed. "And I still haven't heard a reason for you to stay out there."

"Okay, you've got me. I didn't want to admit this, but that couch of yours isn't big enough. And before you say it—"

"I know. You won't take my room." She rolled her eyes. "Well, have it your way until you're ready to tell me the truth." She grabbed an armload of Scott's clothes and went to the closet.

He stacked T-shirts and socks onto the bed and thought again of Tina. Who knew what would have happened if he hadn't walked away from her that day in the cafeteria.

But why should he take the brunt of the blame? As he'd said to her this morning, he might have considered staying in town...if she had told him the truth.

"Layne."

She looked at him over her shoulder. Whatever she saw made her turn to face him. "What's wrong?"

"You know Tina's little boy?"

"Of course, I know Robbie. Tina and Paz bring him into the shop once in a while. He's a little older than Scott, about four."

"Yeah." He set his jaw and stared at her for a moment. Then he demanded, "Did you also know he's my kid?"

Her eyes widened and her mouth dropped open. She clutched the pile of T-shirts she was holding to her chest. "*No*. Why didn't you ever tell me?"

He shrugged. "Didn't know myself till this week."

She put her hand to her mouth to cover her gasp. Her eyes filled with tears.

He looked away. He knew Layne. She wasn't faking her responses. Any thoughts he might have had about her keeping the truth from him disappeared.

"Oh, Cole, I'm sorry." She leaned against the closet door frame. "I can't… I just… I don't know what to say."

"I didn't mean to dump this on you right away. Or at all. You've got enough to worry about."

"Don't be silly. You're my big brother. Cole…how could she not tell you?"

"We were together only once. By the time I could have seen she was pregnant, I was already gone."

She shook her head. "I had no idea. Well…I might have wondered how much you liked her, but I never thought you'd slept with her."

"You'd never heard folks talking?" He forced a laugh. "After all, you work in the biggest gossip mill in New Mexico."

"People talked about it when she got pregnant. They wondered. You know how Tina is, always so quiet. So private."

"Yeah." Quiet and calm, never feeling the restlessness he did. Never wanting to go anywhere outside Cowboy Creek.

"I'll bet no one ever asked her who Robbie's father was. Not even Sugar."

"Maybe she did but wouldn't tell you, since I'm your brother."

Immediately, she shook her head. "No. You know how Sugar is, too. And she's such good friends with Paz and Jed. She'd have been all over me to get you back here to do the right thing." Again, she tried to cover her gasp. "I'm sorry. That wasn't what I was thinking. I meant that's what she would say."

"Don't worry about it," he said grimly. "It's nothing I haven't thought already."

"Would you have settled down, if you'd known?" she asked. "With Tina?"

"Marry her?" He'd never told Layne just how close he'd come to that with another woman. He shook his head. "I'm not marriage material. But all the folks around here would expect a man to do just that."

He thought about what Tina had said this morning.

I'm the trustworthy one standing here. I'm the one who doesn't run from responsibility.

Hadn't that been just what he'd done when he'd walked away from Garland Ranch without giving notice? And then when he'd left town and never looked back?

He wasn't about to do that now.

Maybe he didn't have what it would take to be his son's daddy. But he had to try.

As if she had read his thoughts, Layne said softly, "What are you going to do?"

"For now, get to know the boy."

And that was only his first step.

His apology to Jed had reinforced the decision he'd already made, before he had even known he'd had a son.

He would never again walk away from anywhere—or from anyone—without taking responsibility for his actions.

Chapter Seven

Cole had stayed at Layne's for the night, then packed up his duffel bag and tossed it into the pickup, ready for his move to Garland Ranch.

He walked past the corral on his way to the barn and, as usual, his gaze went toward the hotel. Judging by the couple of cars in the parking area, business must have picked up since yesterday. The Hitching Post could have guests for him to entertain at supper tonight. He shook his head over Jed's idea.

At least the plan would buy him more time with his son.

No doubt Tina would be around, too. He hoped he'd have better luck handling the upcoming encounters with her than he had getting her out of his mind last night. Anger had fueled most of his thoughts, until his teenaged memories of her had started to surface. Memories he didn't want to think about right now.

Inside the barn, he found his new manager in the small office at a desk piled high with paperwork.

When Pete saw him in the doorway, he gestured toward the heel-scuffed stool that had always served as a guest seat. "Take a load off." He looked at his desk and grimaced. "There's no job on earth I'd rather have than running a ranch. But I guess you always have to take the good with the bad."

"True enough."

"Speaking of which..." Pete shoved aside a stack of folders and rested his elbows on the desk.

"What's up? Are you giving me my walking papers already?" The thought bothered him more than it should have. He was used to moving from ranch to ranch. He preferred it that way.

"No, nothing like that. Work got out of hand last week, and I never had the chance to say I'm sorry for the reason you're back in town. It's gotta be rough for your sister, out on her own now with her boy and another kid on the way."

"Yeah, she's having a tough time. But she'll be fine."

"I'm sure she will."

According to what Jed had told him, Pete had gone through a tough time, too. The ranch manager and his wife had split up, leaving him with custody of his kids. Another single parent like Layne.

And Tina.

What had life been like for her after he'd left? She'd been pregnant, with not even her closest relatives to confide in and with the father of her baby nowhere in sight. Keeping her secret from Jed and Paz had been her decision. As for the rest...

Well, she'd made the choice to keep the news from him, too.

He focused on Pete again. "I hear you've got kids now, one of each. Can't be too easy on you, either, taking care of them alone."

"Most of the time, it's harder on them than it is on me." The other man ran his hand through his hair and sighed. "But I sure can't call it a ride in a pony cart, I'll tell you that. Especially now my daughter, Rachel, asks so darned many questions. She's a smart kid, though, for being only five."

Hearing the pride in Pete's tone made him want to brag on his own son. But Tina's decision meant *he* had to keep quiet, too.

"Between the pair of them," Pete continued, "they keep me hopping."

"I think Layne's feeling the same thing."

"Yeah. Luckily, she's now got you to take up some of the slack." Pete grinned. "I hear you're practically a professional nanny to her boy."

"I wouldn't go that far. But I'm helping out since her ex is backtracking as fast as he can." Scowling at the memory, he explained, "He was supposed to pick up her son last night, take him out for ice cream. That never happened."

"Not a big surprise. Terry was hired on here for a short time after you'd left. A *real* short time. He wasn't the most reliable of wranglers. And you know the boss doesn't put up with any crap."

Yet, Jed had shaken his hand in friendship and taken him on again even after he'd walked out years ago. Then the man had given him a room in his hotel.

"Anyway," Pete went on, "the situation with Terry brings me to my second point. As you're the only wrangler living off the ranch with family, I'll do my best to get you out of here on time at the end of the day."

"I appreciate that, but I was planning to tell you this morning. I've moved. For now, Jed's putting me up at the hotel."

Pete whistled. "Nice. But better not let any of the boys hear about it, or we'll have a lynch mob on our hands."

"Hey, how can they complain? There's no room in the bunkhouse."

"Where'd you hear that?"

"Jed."

Pete's brows shot up, but he only nodded and shifted

the conversation to their jobs for the day. Pretty good control, since obviously the announcement had thrown him.

Pete's reaction confirmed what Tina had claimed. Normally, ranch hands didn't bunk in at the hotel.

Jed had pulled a fast one. Which only reinforced Cole's feeling there was something strange going on around here.

Tina stood at the kitchen sink to rinse the plates Robbie and Trey had used for their afternoon snack.

At the counter beside her, Abuela diced green peppers on a cutting board, the steady *chop-chop* familiar to Tina's ears. As a child, when she wasn't upstairs in her attic hideaway, she was often down here in the kitchen with Abuela, doing homework, chatting, asking questions.

In a way, the tables had just been turned. She had spent half her time in the kitchen with the boys, answering Robbie's questions about Scott. How long would it be before he began asking about Cole, especially once the man moved into the hotel later today?

Abuela slid the peppers into a bowl and began chopping onions. The strong scent made Tina's eyes water.

"Those boys play well together," Abuela said.

"Yes, they do." She was glad for that.

"I think Robbie is happy to have other little boys in the hotel. Maybe Cole will bring Scott back again."

"Maybe." She hesitated, then said, "Do you know why Jed fired Cole?"

Abuela looked at her. "*Fired?* Jed did no such thing. Cole left on his own."

Tina stared back. She had always thought Jed had a reason for letting Cole go. But he had never said and she had never felt she could ask. "Do you know why he left Cowboy Creek?"

"No."

She watched Abuela's steady hands. The soothing rhythm let her mind wander.

Since she couldn't find answers to her questions about Cole right that moment, her thoughts went to her son. Robbie had never asked her about his father. That day would come, and probably soon.

She hadn't been much older than Robbie when she had begun questioning Abuela about her parents.

Why don't I have a mama and a daddy? Where did they go? Why don't they love me?

Tina brushed at her eyes. Abuela looked up from her cutting board. Tina laughed and pointed to the onions, then moved a step away to lean against the sink.

When she had asked those questions aloud, Abuela's eyes had always filled with tears. Too distraught to respond, she would call on Jed to provide the answers Tina wanted.

He had long ago explained that her father—his son—had left Cowboy Creek before she was born. Her mother had followed him within days after giving birth, leaving her for Abuela and Jed to raise. Neither of her parents had ever returned to Cowboy Creek. But until Abuela had needed Jed's help to register her for school, even he hadn't known she was his granddaughter.

"Jed's happy to have the girls and Andi's children visit." Abuela sighed. "It's hard for him when he doesn't see them." She looked up from her work to smile at Tina. "I am so thankful I have you and Robbie right here with me."

"So are we." She linked her fingers in front of her and stared down at them. "Abuela...why did you wait so long to tell Jed I was his granddaughter?"

The knife stilled on the cutting board. After a moment, Abuela said, "I was afraid."

"Of Jed?"

"Never of Jed. But for my job. I needed my income to take care of you."

"And you've always done that. You've always been here for me." She had to swallow hard before she could continue. "Did you really think Jed would fire you?"

"I didn't know." Abuela slid the onions into the bowl with the peppers and reached for the plastic wrap. "I'd been here only a short time. Once his son left town, Jed was upset, and I didn't know how he would feel if I told him. It was foolish maybe, but I decided I couldn't take the chance." She set the covered bowl into the cavernous refrigerator, then closed the door with a heavy thump.

Tina could almost feel her grandmother's need to get away. But there was one more question she had to ask. "Abuela…"

"Yes?" She stood gripping the door handle.

"Did you think Jed wouldn't want to know the truth?"

"Don't say that." Her voice broke. She turned to Tina, her eyes brimming with tears. "That makes me feel more guilt than I already do. Of course he would want to know." She crossed the room and clasped Tina's hands in hers. "It's true I didn't tell Jed until later. But that makes no difference to him. Don't ever forget that, *querida*. He loves you just as much as he loves all his family. The same way—" Again, her voice broke.

"I know," Tina said, hugging her tight. "The same way you've always loved me."

TINA SAT AT the kitchen table and ruffled the edges of the hand-woven place mat in front of her without seeing it. Abuela had gone to the dining room to make sure everything was in place for dinner. The waitress on the afternoon shift would already have done that. But as always when their conversations wandered into the past, Abuela felt the need to escape.

After a while, Tina had learned to take those conversations directly to Jed. He always had answers—except when she asked what had happened to her parents after they left. Not even he could tell her that, until notice had come of their deaths in an auto accident when she was twelve.

JED WALKED INTO the kitchen. She jumped at the sight of him. She had been so caught up in her thoughts, she hadn't heard his footsteps.

"Didn't mean to startle you." He poured himself a cup of coffee, then took his usual seat at the table. "The girls won't be here long, you know. How are you all coming along with the plans?"

"We haven't gotten too far," she admitted.

"You'll need to get a move on, then." She watched him take a sip from his mug. Abuela was right. He looked happy. Pleased with himself. Or maybe with Jane and Andi. So far, he had gone right along with every suggestion they had made.

Ally would tease her for being too much of an accountant, but she kept the books and knew their financial situation better than Jed did. She disliked having to remind him of the bottom line with this project. Yet wasn't that exactly why he had chosen her for this new role?

"You know, Abuelo, the ranch has always made a profit, but that's not true for the hotel. We don't have a lot of capital to sink into extensive renovations. Andi and Jane... Well, they don't have much experience working with budgets." That was the kindest way she could think of to phrase it.

The girls' parents had never hurt for money, which

meant neither had they. And over the years, that hadn't changed.

Andi had married into a wealthy family and still lived with her husband's relatives in Arizona. Jane was based in New York City but traveled all over the world for her well-paying job. During their brief meeting in the dining room, her cousins had acted as if they'd never before heard the word *budget*.

The renovations might be meant to help Jed fulfill his dream, but his other granddaughters' costly suggestions were giving her nightmares.

"Don't get yourself worked up, girl," he said. "We'll worry about money when we get to that stage. You know I'm good for going with the flow."

That was just what she feared. As down-to-earth as Jed could be, he sometimes fell short in the planning stages. Ally wouldn't hesitate to tell her she did too much planning, but still, there were some things even she couldn't anticipate.

She thought of Jed's claim that he wanted to provide live entertainment for his guests. That little brainstorm was interfering with her sleep, too. Even she would admit the idea had potential. But why had he chosen the ranch's newest hire to be their resident cowboy?

Cole had returned to town after five years away. Andi and Jane, Jed's "surprise," hadn't visited for a while until now, either. And yet, here they were, too. An odd coincidence.

Or was it?

Had the timing not been accidental at all?

"Abuelo," she said, "speaking of going with the flow… this thought of yours about inviting a cowhand into the dining room—"

"Yeah, an inspiration, wasn't it? I don't know why I never thought of it before."

"I don't know, either. Or why you've thought of it now." She looked him in the eye. "Jed, are you up to something?"

"Me? What makes you ask that?" He rose to take his mug to the sink.

She frowned. He'd sounded so surprised. So innocent. "I don't know. Giving Cole a job on the ranch when he hasn't been back in town for years... And then inviting him to stay in the hotel, when you've never done that with any employee... It makes me think you've got an ulterior motive."

"Not an ulterior one. A *profit* motive. That ought to make you happy. I'm thinking about what's good for business, that's all." He smiled. "Speaking of which, we'll have our new guests lining up for their first riding lesson tomorrow. You'll give Pete a hand?"

She wanted to raise the issue about Cole and her cousins, but with nothing to support her suspicions, how could she?

"Of course I'll help Pete. As always." Jed claimed she provided a calming presence in the corral for all their guests, especially the children. She didn't mind. She loved to ride and loved working with kids, and helping out with the lessons got her out of the house. "'You can't sit at your desk all day, every day,'" she teased, repeating the comment he often made to her.

"That's my girl. I knew you'd start seeing reason sooner or later."

After he had left the room, she sighed, wishing he would see reason about her cousins' ideas for the Hitching Post.

She thought of having to tell Jed and Abuela the truth about Robbie's daddy. Her cousins would find out eventually, too, but her grandparents needed to be the first ones she told. At last.

Confessing once would take all the courage she had. She couldn't hold that conversation a second time. When she talked to Abuela and Jed, she wanted them both together. And not in this room. It was never easy to get Abuela away from her kitchen for any length of time, but this certainly wasn't the best place for a private chat.

She dreaded having to share the news even now. Especially now, as she'd kept her secret from them for so many years. Abuela would be shocked at learning about Cole and hurt by her long silence. And Jed—who had always loved her, just as Abuela had said—would be hurt, too. They both loved Robbie as much as they loved her.

She rose to transfer the few dishes from the sink into the dishwasher. To wipe down every already immaculate counter in the room. To do anything that would provide a distraction from her thoughts.

Someone was bound to walk in here at any moment, and she now had no onions handy to blame for her tear-filled eyes.

For Tina, dinner at the Hitching Post was fast becoming the most uncomfortable meal she could ever remember.

Shortly before they had sat down to eat, she had been finishing up some emails in her office. She had heard boot steps on the hardwood floor of the lobby and looked up to find Cole leaning against the door frame. After his day on the ranch, he had showered and dressed in nearly full cowboy attire, down to and including fringed chaps.

As she looked him over and raised her brows, he had grinned. "Might as well give the crowd a thrill. I'd have worn spurs, too, if I didn't think Paz would have my hide for it."

"Abuela wouldn't be too happy if you scratched the furniture," she had agreed.

Now *she* wasn't at all happy watching him charm everyone in the dining room.

But he had always been Cole Slater, the playboy. The boy who had once had her under his spell. The boy whose magic had ultimately proved to be an act full of smoke and mirrors. A well-practiced act, like the one he was performing now.

Yet, somehow he seemed different tonight. More relaxed. More genuine. More sincere than the boy she had known years ago.

And definitely sexier than ever.

Startled, she stared down at her plate. Where had that thought come from? And what had she done with all her common sense? One show of weakness in front of Cole could give him an advantage over her. Again.

Almost against her will, she found herself looking in his direction. She sat and she watched and she worried as he played the role of cowpoke to the hilt. Or rather, to the shiny silver buckle on his belt. A buckle, he'd told their guests, he had won at a rodeo in Abilene. Then he'd proceeded to regale them with tales of his bull-riding days.

The guests weren't the only ones wide-eyed and plying him with questions.

"Y-you killed a animal?" Robbie asked, his bottom lip quivering.

"No," Cole said immediately. "I just tested my skill against those bulls. Like this—here." He took a dinner roll from the basket in front of him and tossed it underhand toward Robbie.

Robbie grabbed the roll between his palms and grinned.

Cole smiled back at him. "See how fast you caught that? Those bulls are fast, too. I wanted to see how long I could stay on 'em before they threw me off. It's a lot different from riding a horse."

"Like Bingo?" Robbie asked.

Bingo was the smallest pony in Jed's stable. Before Tina could respond, Cole answered.

"Yeah, like Bingo. He's your horse, huh?"

"Yep. He's little, like me. But Scott's littler. If Scott comes sometimes, I can ride Shadow. Right, Grandpa?"

"Sure you can. You're getting plenty big enough for Shadow. Now, you see?" Jed looked at the guests seated at two of the smaller tables. "If my little guy can handle himself on a horse, we'll have y'all up in the saddle in no time."

Tina noticed he was careful not to let his gaze linger on the elder of the couples. When they had checked in and he had mentioned horseback riding, Mr. Dunbar had responded enthusiastically, but his wife had said nothing.

Trust Jed to find a way of offering reassurances kindly, and without making an issue of it.

Just as Cole had done with Robbie.

She thought of her conversation in the kitchen that afternoon, of the question she had asked Abuela.

Did you think Jed wouldn't want to know the truth?

From the minute Cole had met her son, she had watched his reactions. She had read the anger in his posture. Had heard the hurt in his tone. At this moment, she could see the wonder in his eyes.

Every single emotion said he would have wanted to know about Robbie.

Chapter Eight

After dinner ended, Cole asked Robbie about his ponies. When her son enthusiastically led him down the hall, with Trey toddling behind them, Tina found herself trailing along, too.

To keep an eye on the boys, she told herself. And of course, to visit with their guests.

She and Jed always kept themselves accessible to those who stayed in the hotel. They made a point of joining their guests for a while in the sitting room during the afternoons and evenings. When Abuela was free after dinner, she often stopped in before going to her room in their family wing of the hotel. Now Cole would be there, too.

In the sitting room, she settled into her favorite chair and pulled the afghan from the back of it into her lap. Less than three feet from her, Cole took a seat on the floor in front of the couch. The boys hurried to the corner where they had left the plastic horses.

To her dismay, all four of the hotel's guests crossed the reception area without even a glance into the sitting room. A moment later, they closed the front door behind them. Then she heard Jed in the hallway directing Jane and Andi to his den.

She had expected Jed, at least, to come in here. Instead, she was alone with the two boys and Cole.

From the cubby built into the coffee table, he pulled out a wicker basket filled with her son's building blocks. Idly, he stirred through them.

The chunking sound caught Robbie's attention. Leaving the ponies behind, he and Trey came to kneel beside Cole. Robbie tilted the basket, spilling blocks onto the floor.

"We can make a dungeon," he said. "Or a castle or a fort." He tilted his head and looked at Cole. "But no corral, okay?"

"No corral, pardner. If that's the way you want it."

He sat watching Robbie and Trey.

Cuddled beneath her afghan, Tina watched Cole. Again.

Occasionally, he would offer the boys a helping hand when a block got away from them or their fort threatened to collapse.

Right now, she felt about as shaky as their structure. She prided herself on her logic and ran her life based on careful analyses. But like the boys' blocks, her emotions were getting away from her.

The sight of Cole and Robbie smiling at each other made her chest tighten and her eyes prickle. Made her think how much different things could have been...if Cole hadn't walked away from her, causing her to pull her reserve around her like the afghan she now had tucked nearly under her chin.

Things could have been different, too, if Cole hadn't left.

But he *had* left—first his job here at the ranch and then Cowboy Creek altogether—without giving her time to find a way to tell him about her pregnancy.

Yet in all honesty, how could she put one hundred percent of the blame on him?

Suppose you'd given me the news a long time ago? he

had asked. *How do you know I wouldn't have stayed in town then?*

He'd said nothing about staying *with her*.

She was the one with the long-held dreams of settling down with him someday.

Dreams it seemed she couldn't forget even now.

Until this week, she hadn't spoken to Cole for so long. She had no idea what kind of man he had become, except the kind who would help two small children build a fort from wooden blocks. The kind who would reassure a frightened little boy who cared about animals.

After Cole had left town, she and Ally had never worked up the nerve to question his sister about him. They hadn't felt they could ask Sugar or even Abuela. As a result, she had never known his reasons for leaving Cowboy Creek.

She also knew nothing about what he had done in all the time he'd been gone. But now she had both the nerve and the need to ask. For Robbie's sake.

Cole looked at the chime clock on the wall, then up at her from his seat on the floor. "I'm not keeping you from anything important, am I?"

"No. Why?"

"Just thought you might have something better to do than supervise this construction site."

She couldn't miss the edge in his voice. "Nothing better than keeping an eye on things. In case you suddenly decide to break free of this corral."

Robbie looked up. "No corrals, Mama. Not for the ponies." He turned to Trey. "The ponies!" he said, as if suddenly remembering the herd they had left in the corner of the room. Within seconds, the boys had abandoned the blocks for the horses.

His eyes narrowed. "You heard me say that the other day."

"I did. Is that why you left town in the first place? You wanted to break free?"

He stayed quiet for so long that she thought he wouldn't answer.

"One of the reasons," he said finally.

"Layne never mentioned what you've been doing since you've been gone."

"Cowhand."

The same work Jed had hired him to do, now and years ago.

She could envision Cole in those high school days as if no time had passed at all.

While she rode the county bus home, he had driven his pickup truck, which meant he arrived at the ranch much sooner than she did. So many times, Abuela had scolded her for running right to the barn once the bus had dropped her off when she should have gone inside to tackle her homework and chores. But she had lived in hope that she could steal a few minutes to talk with him before he started his assigned job for the afternoon.

"Did you go somewhere in particular?" she asked.

He shook his head. "No. I didn't want to get tied down." For a moment, his eyes looked bleak. He set one of the building blocks on top of another and batted it off again. "A rolling stone, that's me. Meant to roam. I stayed in the South, though. Spent the last two years in Texas. It's a big state."

"As nice as New Mexico?"

He laughed. "Talk to my friends in Dallas, and they'll tell you everything's bigger *and* better in Texas."

"Nothing's better than being home." When he didn't respond, she asked, "What are your plans now?"

He shrugged. "To give Layne a hand."

Not the most definitive answer. She couldn't push without being willing to give in return if he pushed back. And she wasn't ready for that. Instead, she said, "This was the first I'd heard about her having to move."

"She didn't get much warning, either."

His grim expression made her wince.

"I don't see her very much anymore," she admitted, "not even at SugarPie's. Abuela and I stop there when we go into town to grocery shop. But it always seems to be a day Layne's not there. I'm sorry things didn't work out for her and Terry."

"She's better off."

"From her situation with Terry or from marriage in general?"

If she had given herself time to think, she would never have spoken. Why bother, when she already knew what his answer would be? But now she *had* asked the question, she wouldn't back down.

KNOWING—AND NOT LIKING—the direction their conversation had suddenly taken, Cole stared back at Tina. "What does that mean?" he asked, keeping his voice low.

"The first day you came in to the hotel, you made a comment about swearing off marriage and kids."

"Yeah. I made that statement about me, not Layne. And before I knew I had a son. That changes part of the equation."

He stacked a couple of blocks in front of him. He'd barely spent any time at all with the boy. Certainly not enough time to figure out how to break the news to him. And right now he wasn't thinking beyond that.

Obviously, she wasn't any more prepared.

One of them needed to redirect this conversation.

"Speaking of changing things," he said, "how are you feeling about all the excitement around here?"

At yesterday's brunch, when Andi had arrived and Jed had made his big announcement about the hotel, he could tell Tina hadn't liked the news at all. He felt sure no one else had noticed. But he had sat right beside her, close enough to hear her breath catch. Close enough to see the way she had clamped her hands together beneath the edge of the table.

From Jane and Andi's comments at supper tonight, he knew she was doing her part, keeping track of ideas for the hotel in order to gather estimates for the work.

Still, she seemed quieter about the project than he had ever known her to be about anything.

And she hadn't responded to his question. She probably never would, unless he could break through that reserve of hers. He knew what would do it. And—what the heck—it wouldn't hurt to make clear how he stood on a subject she had raised herself.

"To tell you the truth," he said, "I don't see a problem with the hotel the way it is. But then, I'm not much for weddings, especially after what happened at mine."

Her eyes opened wide. "You're married?"

"Was, almost."

She frowned. It didn't take long for her analytical mind to figure out the answer. "You mean, you were engaged?"

"Yeah, for a short time. Until I found myself standing in front of a Las Vegas preacher with no bride."

"Someone left you at the altar?" She sounded stunned.

"Truthfully, I don't think the place had an altar. But yeah, she stood me up. And I deserved it. I should have known better." And he'd learned from the experience. It had been his first—and sure as hell his last—attempt at marriage.

"That," he said, "explains why I'm not much into the

idea of turning this into a honeymoon hotel. What's your objection?"

"What makes you think I object?"

"Call it a reluctance, then. A difference of opinion. An unwillingness to take one for the team."

She winced. "I'm not unwilling. It's just that...I was raised here. The Hitching Post is more than a hotel. It's my home. And I don't like the idea of making drastic changes to it."

Suddenly, he felt an urge to smile. That statement of hers took him back quite a few years.

Tina had never liked change or anything that upset her carefully thought-out plans. From kindergarten till now, she had held the same interests, going so far as to turn her favorite school subject into her full-time job. She had kept the same hairstyle, that long braid she hadn't let him unravel the night they'd...

Well, no sense thinking about that.

The point was, she had stayed the same quiet, reserved Tina she'd always been. An all-business bookkeeper with a soft heart when it came to houses and kids.

Even if he forgot the secret she'd kept—as if he could—she wasn't *at all* the kind of woman a man who had sworn off marriage should be thinking about.

"You're doing fine, Scott," Tina told Cole's nephew the next afternoon. She led him on horseback in a slow walk inside the corral.

"It's bumpy," he said with a nervous giggle.

"I know it is. But you'll get used to being on Bingo. Then it will feel as easy as riding in Uncle Cole's truck." After mentally shaking her head for bringing up the man's name, she attempted to forget him and just enjoy the sunshine soaking into her shoulders.

A failed attempt, since the tingling between her shoulder blades made her certain he was watching her. Again.

She hadn't been a bit happy when she had come out to the barn that afternoon and seen Cole and another hand leading their more seasoned horses into the corral.

When she asked him about it, he told her Pete said Jed had made some changes to the day's roster. Jed had told his manager to pass along the message that Cole should help with the riding lessons.

Her suspicions about Abuelo flared again. But if she asked him, she knew she would get only another seemingly innocent explanation.

The pony tugged on the lead rope in her hand. "Be careful with your feet," she reminded Scott. "If you kick Bingo, he'll think you want to go faster."

He nodded, but then his lower lip trembled.

Her heart went out to him.

Though they had given him the smallest mount in Jed's stable and she had walked his pony for a good hour, he still hadn't gotten comfortable. He glanced enviously at Robbie and at Pete's five-year-old daughter, Rachel, both trotting their horses around the perimeter of the corral and obviously at home in the saddle.

Riding lessons at the ranch included a list of instructions. Their guests watched as their horses were saddled up and learned how to adjust the girth and stirrups, with everything double-checked by the wranglers, of course, before anyone was allowed to ride.

Cole had worked with the adults and now was patiently leading the nervous Mrs. Dunbar on horseback around the corral.

Tina gave the woman an encouraging smile.

As she glanced at Cole, his gaze met hers. For a moment, the several dozen yards between them seemed reduced to a handful of inches.

Unsettled, she turned away.

Last night, his announcement about being left at the altar had shaken her more than it should have, too.

She focused again on the boy astride the pony. "See, Scott," she said, "in the beginning everybody has to learn how to ride. You'll get there."

She spent another few minutes walking him and Bingo inside the fence. Anything to keep her away from Cole. Yet she couldn't resist another peek across the corral.

He had helped Mrs. Dunbar dismount and was handing her horse's reins over to one of the stable hands.

Though her emotions were in a whirl, as she watched him the cool, analytical side of her brain couldn't help taking over, making a quick tally of what she saw.

To the credit column, she added blue eyes the color of a springtime sky. Brown hair as soft as the silk of her favorite nightgown. A generous mouth she unfortunately from time to time still dreamed about. And the entries went on and on.

Too bad the single item in the debit column canceled everything out.

"Hey, Mama," Robbie called, waving from his seat on Shadow.

She waved in return.

"Looking good," Cole called.

He might have meant the compliment for Robbie or Scott or anyone else in the corral. But when she turned, he was striding in her direction. His gaze was firmly on her, making her conscious of her comfy but too-snug jeans and scruffy boots.

Suddenly, she had trouble taking a deep breath, as if the old T-shirt she'd thrown on to wear had shrunk in the wash.

Grinning, he looked her up and down.

Darn Cole.

He was the same irrepressible playboy she had known since grade school, and she had reacted automatically like the love-struck girl she'd been then, too. As she brought Scott and Bingo to a stop beside the corral fence, she gave herself a swift, silent reprimand. The sight of eagle-eyed Jed standing in the barn doorway and the guests nearby also helped focus her.

When Cole reached her, she forced a smile. "He's getting the hang of it," she said. "We'll have him on a trail ride before he knows it."

"I see a rodeo win in his future."

"A champion belt buckle, for sure."

Scott gave a shaky laugh.

"Great riding, pardner," Cole said.

To his credit, he seemed to be doing his best to be a good uncle to his nephew...and to form a bond with both Scott and Robbie. The thought touched her heart at the same time it threw her into a tailspin.

She swallowed hard and looked at the little boy. "Ready to stop for today?"

When he nodded, Cole lifted him out of the saddle, then swung him to the ground on the other side of the fence.

"I ride like the big kids, Uncle Cole!"

"Just like them, all right," he agreed, removing the boy's riding helmet.

Giggling, Scott ran to join Robbie at one of the low benches set a few yards from the corral fence.

She had to swallow hard again before she could speak. "For someone who claims he swore off kids, you're doing a good job."

"I've had a great example to follow." He smiled, his

dimples flashing. "Seriously, Tina, I've never seen anyone as good with kids as you are."

She grimaced. "I'm betting you haven't had much experience watching anyone interact with kids."

"I've seen enough to know you've got a lot of patience."

Giving the lie to his statement, impatience ran through her.

Confusion did, too. She blamed that on the mixed messages she was receiving—from herself.

She didn't want to talk with Cole about her skills with kids. At times, she didn't want to talk to him at all... Inwardly, she winced at that echo of the final night of their long-ago weekend together. The old memory and her fresh guilt made her wish for an escape.

From the corner of her eye, she saw Jed watching them, giving her another much-needed reminder she had a job to do. She forced herself to meet Cole's eyes, the same shade of blue as the sky above them. The same shade as Robbie's.

"Scott did very well," she told him. "He said it was his first time on horseback."

He looked over toward the boys. "I guess Layne never had much time to take him riding."

"It's a shame he isn't comfortable around horses, since he lives in a ranching community. You could help change that."

"Maybe." He kept his focus on the kids. The brim of his Stetson shadowed his eyes, but she could see his profile, the strong curve of his jawline, one corner of his mouth...

She wanted to move closer. Close enough for a kiss.

Instead, she grasped the pony's rope and got a grip on her pride—before it could desert her entirely. "He was starting to enjoy himself, I think. It helped that Pete made sure to give us Bingo."

"Nice Shetland."

"And well broken-in. Rachel and Robbie usually ride him."

He nodded. "So Pete said."

"Well, I think we've wrapped up the lessons for today." As she turned, Cole reached out to stop her.

The temperature that afternoon had risen high for mid-March in New Mexico. Still, she couldn't miss the added warmth from his hand on her arm. She turned to face him again, at the same time managing to slip free of his touch.

"Thank you," he said.

She frowned. "For...?"

"Scott was all fired up this morning about going for a pony ride—till we got here. I saw the panic on his face as we led the horses from the barn. And then I saw how he relaxed when you brought the kids into the corral."

She had noticed Scott's expression, too, and had immediately gone to Pete's house to get Robbie and Rachel. "No problem. Neither of them put up a fuss about riding with the guests. I thought it might help Scott to see the other kids on horseback."

"It did. But I don't think he would have gotten up on this pony without you. Thanks for that, too."

He gave her a genuine smile that left her insides shaky. "You're welcome." She backed a step. "I'd better go unsaddle Bingo."

"I'll do it." As he took the lead rope from her hand, their fingers brushed. He stared at her for a moment, then turned and led the pony away.

She stood watching him and wishing she could make sense of the emotions that had been running through her lately.

A moment ago, she had felt like a teenager in love all over again.

Last night after he had told her about being left at the

altar, for another brief moment she had turned into a jealous teen satisfied at knowing he'd gotten a taste of his own medicine.

Yet a few hours later, long after that tiny burst of teen-aged jealousy had faded, she lay in bed, sleepless at the thought of Cole marrying someone else.

If Ally had learned news like that from a man she cared about, she would probably have thrown something at him and then thrown him out.

That wasn't Tina's way.

And that was the problem.

As the night wore on, she had continued to toss and turn. And to worry.

She had felt stunned once she realized Cole would have wanted to know about Robbie. Watching them together in the sitting room had only added to her guilt. She never should have kept the truth from Cole.

No matter what he had done in the past, he had deserved to know about their child.

Chapter Nine

In her office a few days later, Tina finished checking the supply order that had arrived from their online distributor.

She heard a rapping sound and looked through the doorway. Jane stood on the other side of the registration desk.

Her cousins planned to stay for another week. Until then, she hoped she could keep their ideas for the renovation under control. Except for that worry, she admitted to an advantage to having them around.

Cole ate breakfast and lunch in the bunkhouse with the rest of the wranglers, but if he wasn't in town with Layne, he came to dinner at the Hitching Post. Her cousins unknowingly continued to help run interference between her and Cole.

"Hey," Jane said. "Andi just went to her room with the kids for a minute. As soon as she's down here again, we're ready for that tour you promised us this morning."

"Sounds good." She didn't remind Jane it was Jed who had made the promise. And though she didn't look forward to the tour, she acknowledged the afternoon could provide another advantage. If she heard her cousins' more extravagant ideas before Jed did, she would have a better chance of squashing them.

"I'll be in the sitting room," Jane said.

"Great. And I'll be back in a minute."

She grabbed a stack of order pads and a box of pens from her desk. Then she marched down the hall.

Other than helping with the riding lessons, her trips around the hotel had been the extent of her exercise this week. Ally was working overtime doing inventory at the store, which meant they hadn't been able to get together to walk.

Instead, she had received frantic daily phone calls. Ally was doing her best to get a date with her cute cowboy, who didn't seem to be taking any of her hints. Tina had almost laughed. Though Ally didn't know it, Ally had had more time alone with her cowhand than Tina had had with Cole.

On a couple of the nights Layne was working at Sugar-Pie's, Cole had brought Scott to the hotel for supper. And again to his credit, even with the two younger boys and a handful of adults around, he managed to spend time talking with Robbie.

Seeing them together made her heart beat faster, both from happiness and worry. Cole had the right to spend time with his son. She had admitted that to herself. Yet he had told her he was "meant to roam." He had come back to Cowboy Creek "to give Layne a hand." Neither comment left her reassured he wanted an ongoing relationship with Robbie.

She entered the kitchen, where Abuela and Jed sat at the table talking in low voices.

"Am I interrupting something?"

Startled, they glanced at her and then each other.

Her grandparents had begun to concern her, too. This wasn't the first time this week she had found them in here in quiet conversation, as if they were discussing something they didn't want anyone else to hear.

Abuela rose and went to the sink.

"Just figuring out the grocery list for next week," Jed said, leaning back in his chair.

"Oh, really?" Tina said lightly. She put the pens and order pads in the drawer of the china cabinet. "Since when do you get involved in the menu planning?"

"Since we're having a chuckwagon before the girls head home again."

That made sense. The chuckwagon and campfire supper was always a joint effort. Everyone who worked on the ranch and was around that day pitched in to help.

It was also a huge hit with their guests. They roasted their own hot dogs and marshmallows over the fire, while Pete and the cowhands took care of grilling burgers and steaks. Abuela made the salads and sides, and Tina did whatever she was called upon to do. Jed, of course, acted as master of ceremonies.

What didn't make sense at all was Abuela and Jed huddling over the kitchen table to discuss a menu that seldom varied.

He rose. "It's about time for you to show Jane and Andi around the place, isn't it?"

"About," she agreed.

"I'll just go remind them."

"How could they have forgotten? You only suggested it at lunchtime. I see right through you, Abuelo."

He started. "You do?"

"Of course I do." She laughed. "You want more time with those great-grandkids of yours."

He wrapped his arm around her shoulders and gave her a hug. "You know, I think you're right."

"You shouldn't have to wait long. Jane said Andi will be on her way downstairs with the kids any minute."

"Well, then, why don't we both just head out to the lobby to meet them."

With his arm still around her, he escorted her from the room.

It wasn't till they were halfway down the hall that she realized how smoothly he'd gotten her out of the kitchen. And how odd it was that Abuela hadn't said a single word.

Her steps heavy, Tina led her cousins through the upper floor of the hotel.

"I was right," Jane declared. "This could be a real showplace."

Tina swallowed a sigh. In her eyes, the Hitching Post already was a showplace, one filled with charm and beauty, complete with a long, rich history.

If not for her concern about the way her cousins wanted to change the hotel, she wouldn't have played tour guide. Though Jane and Andi hadn't visited often in the past few years, they had spent plenty of time here during their school holidays and most of their summer vacations.

But to her surprise, all afternoon her cousins had exclaimed over parts of the hotel they had never seen before, pointing out some of the features she thought made her home so special. The handmade furniture and intricately carved headboards in the bridal suites... The deep built-in window seats at either end of the upper halls...

"And those original claw-foot tubs in some of the bathrooms!" Andi exclaimed from behind her.

"Great character," Jane agreed. "I'll have to get some shots of those."

Tina smiled, listening to their chatter and feeling proud as if she owned the property.

While still in grade school, she had begun helping the maids polish that furniture, wash those windows and clean all those tubs and more. None of the chores bothered her and she had never complained. She loved every room and hallway, every nook and cranny of the hotel.

"This must go to the attic," Jane said.

Tina stumbled over her own feet. She had deliberately passed the attic stairs without mentioning them. When she turned back, she found Jane and Andi halfway to the floor above.

She put her hand on the railing and took a deep breath. "There's not much up there," she called.

Their footsteps clattered on the bare floorboards.

Frowning, she trudged up the stairs.

Even years ago, neither Abuela nor Jed had ever cared about making the climb to the unused highest floor of the hotel. With no guest rooms on this level, the maids never felt the need to come here, either. Except for a room designated for storage, she had always had the huge open attic all to herself for a playroom, a library, a dance hall. For whatever her needs and imagination made of it. Eventually, she had turned it into her own private sitting room and library.

As much as she had wanted her cousins' companionship when they visited, she had never once thought about showing them her sanctuary. Now they had invited themselves in.

"Very nice," Andi said. "The dormer windows make it cozy but still allow plenty of headroom."

Jane eyed the rest of the area. "For the crowd Grandpa intends to attract, he'll need to think about remodeling up here, converting all this into guest rooms."

Tina held back a groan. If she had to give up her private space...

But it wasn't *her* space.

Her spirits sank even lower as the women discussed their thoughts for renovations.

"That would mean a substantial investment," she objected.

"As they say, you've got to spend money to make money," Jane said flatly.

"And it's not just about money." Andi turned to Tina. "This is about helping Grandpa achieve his dreams."

But at what price?

If Jed wanted to go along with some of these latest ideas, and no doubt he would, she would face even more trouble ahead. The Hitching Post didn't generate enough income to pay for these kinds of upgrades. But she didn't feel comfortable sharing that with her cousins.

Jane glanced at her watch. "I've got to make a quick phone call."

"Thanks for the tour, Tina," Andi said. "I'd better check in on Grandpa and the kids." She smiled. "I'll bet Cole's downstairs with them by now, too. You'll probably want to look in on all of them."

"*I'll* bet Cole will want to see *her*."

Tina frowned, unsure how to take the comment.

"Grandpa's experienced," Jane continued, "but Cole sometimes has that deer-in-the-headlights look when he's around the boys. I wouldn't mind a shot of that expression."

This week, Jane had spent quite a bit of time watching Cole. Tina swallowed hard. Any flicker of jealousy she might have felt disappeared under a flood of new worry. Was Jane the only one paying attention to Cole's interactions with the kids? Or were Abuela and Jed noticing, too? She thought of those whispered conversations they had been having in the kitchen.

She *had* to tell them the truth before they discovered it on their own.

"Not that I blame him," Jane went on, starting down the stairs. "I don't know anything about kids."

Andi followed on her heels. "I know what you mean about Cole, though. I just don't picture him around kids, either. Of course, I'm still thinking of him when we were all teenagers. He's grown up since then."

"I'm surprised you noticed a difference, cuz." Jane's laugh echoed in the stairwell. "Back then, I always thought you had your eye on someone else."

"And do you remember what I always used to say about thinking too much?"

Jane simply laughed again.

It came as no surprise that her cousins didn't bother to share the inside joke with her. Years ago, they had always kept their secrets.

And who was she to take offense? She now had secrets of her own.

Despite Andi's light tone, she was flushing. The woman even did that beautifully, her pink cheeks making her eyes look more blue.

"See you in a few minutes." Jane continued down the stairs to the next floor.

Tina began to follow.

"Tina, wait," Andi said. She looked down the stairwell. Jane had disappeared from view. "Don't mind Jane," she said in a low tone. She sighed. "It's great having this week to catch up again, but I'm worried about her. She's changed a lot in the past couple of years."

"Has she?"

"Yes. And it's funny. She's as outspoken as ever, yet at the same time she's gotten more introverted. More like you."

"Me?"

Andi smiled. "You were always so quiet whenever we came to visit. You still are."

"I guess I don't have Jane's outspoken side."

"Maybe not. And that could be a good thing." Suddenly, Andi turned solemn. "But it's her quiet side that bothers me. I guess it's not surprising she's changed so much, considering what she does for a living."

Puzzled, Tina frowned. "She's a photographer."

"Yes. A freelancer, which can be a tough enough job, according to some of my friends in the business. They work for themselves, mostly doing portraits and parties close to home. Jane does a lot of work in the fashion industry, especially in New York. But that's not what I meant. She was telling me about some of the other assignments she's had. About some of the places she's been to and the things she's seen. The kids…the conditions…" Her eyes filled with tears. "I don't know how she handles it."

"That sounds awful," Tina murmured, stunned. She always pictured slim, fashion-savvy Jane in fabulous settings with glamorous people.

"It *is* awful. I can see why it makes her introverted part of the time. Why she sometimes seems so…so abrupt and unfeeling, I guess. You know she wasn't always like that." Andi took a deep breath. "Anyhow, what she said about Cole…I don't think she meant anything by the way she said it. Grandpa told us Cole barely knows his nephew. I think somebody ought to give him a medal for trying to make up for lost time. And for what he's doing for all the boys."

Tina stiffened. "All the boys…?"

"Well, I guess I shouldn't speak for your son, only mine. Since Grant died, Trey has been so withdrawn." Andi's voice shook, reminding Tina of how traumatic the past few months had been for her. "Cole's doing a great job making him feel like he fits in."

"Is he?" she murmured.

"Yes. You know how it goes with kids. The little ones all want to feel like 'big' kids. And the older ones don't want to hang out with the younger ones." Andi ran her hand along the stair rail, not meeting Tina's eyes.

Was she attempting to explain what she and Jane had done? Was she saying they hadn't excluded her for any personal reason, but simply because she was a couple of years younger?

"Teenagers feel that way, too, I suppose," Tina said slowly.

"Teenagers, especially. Until they grow up and get over themselves. Maybe if Jane and I had visited more often in the past few years, you'd have seen sooner that we've grown up. Like Cole." Though her cheeks had turned as pink as they had when Jane had teased her in the attic, she smiled tentatively.

Tina hesitated, then smiled back at her.

As she followed Andi down the stairs, her heart felt just a bit lighter...until she thought of what she needed to do now.

AFTER TUCKING ROBBIE in that night, Tina checked the kitchen and found it empty, as she had expected.

She had asked Abuela and Jed to meet her in his den.

They were both waiting for her when she arrived, but she had to pause to take a deep breath before she could step into the room.

Jed rested back in the swivel chair with his fingers laced crossed his middle and his crossed feet propped up on the edge of the desk. Abuela sat on the couch with the almost-finished afghan she was crocheting spread across her lap.

She adjusted the guest chair to face them both.

While she was growing up, the three of them had often gathered here for discussions, taking the same comfortable seats. Tonight, she didn't feel at all comfortable.

"Did you get Robbie set for the night?" Jed asked.

"After a while. He wanted to talk about his ponies more than he wanted to focus on sleep." Even to her ears, her laugh sounded forced. She gripped the arms of the chair.

Jed's head tilted thoughtfully, and he eyed her.

Abuela set down the afghan but still held the crochet hook. She was waiting, possibly trying to think of a reason to leave if the conversation drifted where she never liked it to go.

Tina wished this conversation didn't have to happen at all. Suddenly, she was trembling from head to foot. She took a deep breath and clutched the arms of the chair more tightly. "Even though I told you I wanted to talk with you both, I'm not sure how to start."

"That's easy enough," Jed said. "You know I like to hear everything flat-out straight."

"Yes, I do know. But it's something I've never talked about before. Something I never told you. About me. About Robbie."

Jed and Abuela exchanged a quick glance. Her short, rapid sentences sounded nothing like her, and they realized it.

She took another deep breath, struggling to find the way to explain something so complicated, so emotional. The analytical part of her mind said Jed had already given her the answer.

"All right," she said. "Flat-out straight. When I had Robbie, I never told you who his father was. That was partly because I never planned to let the boy know he'd gotten me pregnant. But now he's found out, and I want you to know who he is." She took another deep breath. "Cole."

Abuela gave a low moan.

"Don't," Tina said. By the time she had moved to the couch, tears were trickling down Abuela's cheeks. "Please, don't cry, Abuela."

"Mi vida." My life.

The familiar endearment and her grandmother's distress made Tina's eyes fill, too.

"Now, this won't get us anywhere," Jed protested. She could hear tears beneath his gruff tone. He grabbed a couple of tissues from the box on the coffee table and gave them each one. "You girls take these and pull yourselves together. I'll go start a pot of tea."

Despite the situation, Tina almost smiled. Abuela didn't like conversations about the past, and Jed couldn't handle tears.

As he closed the door behind him, Tina put her arm around Abuela's shoulders. "I'm sorry I never told you."

"It's not that. I don't like seeing the hurt in your eyes."

"I hurt you and Abuelo."

"And I did the same to you both by not telling Jed about you. It's better for Robbie that Cole knows the truth. Trust me."

She did trust Abuela.

But could she say the same about Cole?

Chapter Ten

Tina left the hotel by the kitchen door and went out to the back porch.

In the days after her talk with Abuela and Jed, she hadn't known what reactions to expect from them once the shock of her announcement had worn off. Reproach, cold shoulders or, on the other hand, even more of the love they had always showered on her and Robbie.

As it turned out, she had noticed no difference at all in the way they behaved with her and Robbie or how they acted toward Cole.

Jed was sitting in a porch rocker, keeping an eye on Robbie and Pete's daughter, Rachel, who were playing by the benches near the corral. Even from here, she could hear their voices raised in whatever game they were playing.

Jane and Andi and her kids had gone into town for lunch, and on the way back to the ranch, they planned to pick up Scott.

"I'll go see how those two are doing," she offered.

"Between me here and Cole over there, we've been making a good job of it. But suit yourself."

She went down the porch steps. As she neared the kids, the noise level of their play increased. Judging by the sounds, they seemed to be pretending to be monsters.

Over by the barn, Cole and another hand stood grooming a couple of the horses.

As she crossed the yard, Cole looked up. He dropped his sponge into his bucket and began to cut across the corral.

Her heart skipped a couple of beats, but her pace didn't falter noticeably. She hoped.

She and Cole had continued to work together while giving the riding lessons, but they hadn't had time to talk the way they had during the first session. In fact, they hadn't had any time alone together since then. She hadn't yet told him her grandparents now knew he was Robbie's father.

He had enough to deal with.

Though, at the moment, as he propped one boot on the lowest rail and smiled at her over the top rail, he looked as though he hadn't a care in the world.

"What do you think?" he asked, gesturing toward Robbie and Rachel.

They had draped an old drop cloth across two of the benches. Except for one gaping area, the edges of the drop cloth had been weighted down with rocks. The sounds of roars and screeches came from beneath the cloth.

"I think I must have watched the wrong channel on television this morning," she said. "They didn't say anything about needing to take cover from a tornado."

"Very funny," Cole said. Looking smug, he explained, "It's not a shelter, it's a cave. They started out as wilderness campers and have gone on to become lions in their den."

"And I'm guessing you came up with the idea?"

"I sure did. Gave them some training in lion roars, too."

"Thanks for that," she said drily. "A word of advice, if you don't mind."

"You're the expert," he said with a grin that made her pulse race.

"When they play indoors, the camping scenario will keep them much quieter."

"Yeah, you've got a point there." More roars almost drowned out his voice. "Hey, guys!"

Rachel and Robbie looked out from beneath the cloth-shrouded benches.

"Lions need to check out the jungle once in a while. It's thataway." He pointed toward the swing set in Rachel's yard.

Roaring, the pair took off in that direction.

He had made good progress with the kids in the past few days. She had to give him that. He was still trying. "The new idea isn't bad. For outdoors, of course. Very inventive."

"I have my moments." He laughed, low and deep and too danged sexy for his own good. And for hers.

She took a step backward. "I need to go talk with Jed."

"Is it me or the lions?"

She stared at him. "What?"

"All of a sudden, you jumped as if something had scared you."

"Oh." Ashamed of the reaction, she forced a smile. "It was the lions. You really did a very good job of training them."

"I'll add it to my résumé." Grinning, he touched the brim of his Stetson.

As she made her way across the yard again, she was conscious of his gaze on her. But by the time she took a seat on the porch step, he had gone back to his work.

She rubbed her temples.

"Your head hurt?" Jed asked. His rocker was just a few feet from her. She turned and smiled at him. A genuine smile.

"Just a bit." The nagging headache had begun what

seemed like days ago, and the conversation with Cole had only made it worse.

He might have plenty to deal with right now, but so did she. Along with everything else, she didn't need to find herself fighting an attraction for him. But that's just what she was doing...had been doing, for longer than she wanted to admit.

"I keep telling you, you work too hard. You need to get together with the girls—"

"—and take them on the next tour." Somehow, he didn't consider that work. "It's on the agenda for this afternoon, Abuelo."

"Good." He smiled in satisfaction and continued rocking.

Of course, he would want Jane to check out any good views for photos for the website. She could understand that. But their destinations for the tour—the wedding chapel and the small cabins adjacent to it—had all been unused for so long, she had hoped Jed wouldn't think to add them to the list for their second tour.

No such luck.

"We'll have things pulled together before we know it," he said.

"Well...yes, but the renovations are going to take some time." And money they didn't have.

"I know that, especially with everything we're fixin' to do. But I'll make sure the girls are ready to do their parts just as soon as you give me the word."

"Good." She struggled to sound enthusiastic.

While he had been captivated by Jane and Andi's ideas for the hotel, she still felt unhappy about the extravagant changes they had proposed. She had a list of her own, this one of local contractors. Maybe fresh paint and new curtains would satisfy her cousins. With luck, they would agree to her modifications of their plans before they shared any other costly ideas with Jed.

When she had tried again to discuss the hotel budget with him, he had almost brushed away her concerns.

"You know," she reminded him, "we haven't got enough in the hotel account to cover everything Jane and Andi have mentioned. Unless you want to take out a bank loan—"

"You know how I feel about borrowed money," he grumbled.

"I do. Then whatever renovations you make will have to be done in stages."

"Yeah, so you said." He nodded. "And as I told you, I've got complete confidence you'll get the job done."

She swallowed a sigh. It wasn't Jed's confidence she would need. But she was in this for him. To pull her weight with the project and to give him his dream. She had to find a way to do that...without putting them into bankruptcy.

"Kids seem to be having a good time out there."

"Yes." She looked again at the "den" they had made. Then her gaze went to Cole.

"You and Cole seem to be hitting it off, too."

She straightened. "Has he said that?"

"Nope. Didn't have to. My eyes might not work as well as they once did, but I can still see things that happen right in front of my nose. And what I saw just now was the two of you getting along just fine. Maybe we'll need that wedding chapel ready sooner than you think."

Her vision blurred as she stared out toward the barn. She tried to respond, but her throat felt so tight, she wasn't sure she could swallow, let alone say a word.

Long seconds later, she finally managed to find her voice. "I knew something was up with you, Jed." Resting back against the porch rail, she turned to face him.

"You're the most wonderful man I know, and you have a bigger heart than anyone I've ever met. But it wasn't just out of the goodness of your big heart that you hired Cole and asked him to stay here in the hotel, was it?"

He wouldn't meet her eyes.

She rose and walked over to stand beside the rocker.

After a moment, he looked up. Deep lines bracketed his blue eyes.

She rested her hand on his shoulder and leaned down to kiss his forehead. "Don't worry, Abuelo. I know you and Abuela want everything to work out right for Robbie. But that's something only Cole and I can handle. And I need you to step back and let us handle it."

Unfortunately, as sincere as it had been, that last comment only made her recall the way she had stepped back from Cole.

FOOTSTEPS IN THE lobby followed by the sound of familiar female voices alerted Cole that Tina and her cousins had returned to the hotel. He rested against the sitting room sofa, crossed his arms over his chest and stretched his legs out in front of him, ankles crossed. And he waited.

The three women had taken a trip around the hotel the day before. Today, Jed told him, they had expanded the tour, going outside to inspect the wedding chapel and a couple of the small cabins situated near the hotel.

When the women reached the registration desk, he saw Tina wielding a notepad and pencil like a shield and a dangerous weapon. Still, her expression looked a little less guarded than usual.

Other than their brief conversation yesterday, they hadn't had time alone again since the afternoon at the corral a few days ago. And what an afternoon that had been.

He'd had plenty of time to get a good view of her as

she'd walked the pony around the enclosure. Plenty of opportunities to watch that long braid of hers switching back and forth across hips covered in tight-fitting jeans. For a while there, his body had gotten so tight below his belt, he hadn't trusted he could walk normally.

Then later, they had talked and he had seen the look in her eyes. As always, they told him everything she had on her mind. That afternoon, they had been saying she wasn't nearly as immune to him as she pretended.

But that was a road he had no intention of traveling, no matter how much he liked the view ahead.

What he needed with Tina was a cordial relationship. And some time to finally take care of their current business.

The three women entered the room.

"Everything's looking good in here," Jane said.

"Yep. Things are just fine."

Layne had taken extra hours at SugarPie's tonight, so he had gone into town to pick up his nephew. The three boys had a car race underway in the lobby. They sent their cars zooming past the women and into one corner of the sitting room.

"A man who knows what he's doing around kids," Andi said. "I'm impressed."

"Thank you, ma'am." He grinned.

Tina said nothing. She looked peeved, but whether at her cousins' comments or his responses, he didn't know.

The other two women settled into a couple of chairs, which left Tina on her feet in the doorway and the couch beside him wide open. He patted the cushion. "No sense standing," he told her. "It'll make conversation awkward."

Andi and Jane had their backs toward her, which left her free to shoot daggers at him with her eyes.

Still, she came to take the seat beside him.

Making sure to keep his gaze focused on the other women, he said, "To tell you the truth, I'm pretty impressed with myself. And I'm feeling the need to celebrate."

He put his arm around Tina's shoulders in a very brotherly way, much as he would have with Layne.

Nothing at all like with his sister, she trembled.

Oh, yeah. Not nearly as immune to him as she let on.

"With all the help Tina's given me with the kids, I really feel I ought to take her out for supper."

Beneath his arm, her shoulders went rigid.

"That's a great idea," Andi said. "Why don't you go tonight? Jane and I can watch the boys."

"Me?" Jane asked.

"Yes, you. We need the time together, anyhow. We still have a lot to catch up on."

"No," Tina blurted. "I mean, thanks, but there's no need for Cole to take me out to dinner."

"Oh, there's definitely a need." He waited till she looked at him. "We have a lot to catch up on, too."

"Go ahead, Tina," Andi urged.

Tina leaned down to pick up a car that had rolled to a stop against the coffee table. As she moved, his hand trailed across her shoulders. He didn't care for her skill in slipping away from him. And he enjoyed the touch more than he should have.

Both reactions told him how much he'd been fooling himself. He wanted to go down that road with the tempting view.

"Thanks," she said to the women, "but you're both here to visit, not to work. You're doing enough already with planning for the renovations."

Andi laughed. "Don't worry about it. You know no matter what I said to Jane, Grandpa will be doing most of the work watching the kids. Which reminds me, I really ought to give him a break now. If I can find him." She stood.

"Check the kitchen," Cole told her.

Jane's face lit up. "Then, I'll go with you. Paz might still have some of that cheesecake we had for lunch. And we'll let her know we'll have two fewer people at dinner tonight."

The minute they were left alone—except for the boys in the lobby, of course—Tina jumped up as if the couch had caught fire. Hands on her hips right where he wanted to put *his* hands, she glared at him. "You didn't give me a chance to say no," she said in a low voice.

"That's right. Me or your cousins. They know a good idea when they hear one."

"You'd be surprised how unworkable their ideas are. So is this one. You should have stopped at the lion's den."

Damn. She'd also perfected the skill of throwing a low blow.

"Unworkable?" He shrugged. "I was thinking my ideas were just the opposite. As in the way I'm putting in hours at my day job. Bringing Scott here to hang out with the boys. Spending time with him while I'm getting to know Robbie. That was the deal, wasn't it?"

She didn't respond.

"Besides, we've got the sitters all lined up." He tried for a smile. "So, tell me, ma'am, what's your pleasure for this evening?"

Chapter Eleven

Tina watched as Cole grimaced and ran his thumb along the edge of his plate.

"I don't believe this," he muttered.

"You wanted this," she countered, swallowing a nerve-induced giggle.

He looked at her thoughtfully. "You always give a man—"

—*what he wants?*

The words hung in the air. She knew exactly why he had cut himself off. Unwilling to help him, she said nothing. But she wondered. Putting his arm around her as they'd sat on the couch at the Hitching Post... Insisting they needed to catch up...

Just what did *he* want from *her*?

The thought made her grab her glass of sweet tea for something steady to hold on to. She couldn't believe this situation, either. Dinner. A night out. A *date* with the father of her child—the man who had once left her in the dust.

She had accepted his invitation for an entire list of reasons. Not analytical reasons, she was ashamed to admit, but a list of purely emotional *ifs*.

If Andi and Jane hadn't pressed her, insisting they would babysit and claiming they needed the time to reconnect.

If that statement hadn't once again left her on the outside looking in at them.

If turning down Andi's perfect excuse for her to accept Cole's invitation wouldn't have made her look foolish.

If Jane's interest in the man who now sat across from her hadn't brought to life the teeniest bit of green-eyed jealousy.

And if, heaven help her, her reunion with Cole hadn't unleashed feelings she found impossible to push away. Conflicting feelings that bounced between one emotional extreme and the other. At one end, spine-strengthening pride. At the opposite end, raging, fingertip-tingling, butterflies-in-the-stomach desire.

Cole pushed his plate away and scooted his chair closer to hers.

Her throat tightened, but she couldn't seem to lift her glass of sweet tea. Praying she would survive this evening, she met his gaze.

"I'd have taken you someplace in Albuquerque or Santa Fe," he said. "Heck, I'd have settled for a restaurant here in town, limited though our options might be. And you wanted supper at the Lucky Strike."

"Of course," she said, widening her eyes. "They have the best burgers in the county."

He muttered under his breath.

"Yummy, Uncle Cole," Scott said.

"The best," Robbie agreed.

"Yeah," Rachel said, rolling her eyes. "But are you finished yet?"

The three kids looked expectantly at Cole. Tina bit her lip to hide her smile.

"I am now," he said evenly. "Let's go pick out some bowling balls."

"Yeah!"

The metallic screech as the kids shoved their chairs away from the table barely registered over the noise in the crowded snack bar.

"We were lucky to get a lane reservation," she said brightly as she and Cole followed the kids. "The Bowl-a-Rama always draws a crowd on league nights."

"Yeah, I remember that. The place to be in Cowboy Creek."

"Yes." But not the place to be *for them* as a couple.

Starting in grade school, all the kids had bowled together in groups. Later, they started pairing off. She and Cole were never a pair. Technically, tonight, they were more like part of a team.

And that was her most important reason for accepting Cole's invitation. As she'd told him on their way into the building, she was upholding her end of the deal and giving him another opportunity to be with Robbie.

In her heart, she hoped for a chance at so much more for her son. For herself. For them all.

When Scott ran to the lane to throw his first ball down the alley, Cole came to sit beside her. Close beside her... in the row of molded plastic seats that couldn't be moved or even shifted.

She refused to back away, as she had at the corral yesterday.

She pretended to watch Scott, yet she couldn't focus on anything but the man beside her. Her senses seemed hyperfocused on everything about him. The sight of his sturdy hand and strong, tanned forearm contrasting with the crisp, white fabric of the Western shirt he had rolled up almost to his elbow. The touch of his sleeve and the heat beneath it against her shoulder. The heady scent of his aftershave. The sound of his laugh... That same laugh that had sent her skittering away from him. That low, deep, sexy laugh that made her pulse pound.

She missed only the sense of taste—and she would go on missing it, too. Tasting Cole wasn't on the Lucky Strike's menu.

Robbie's first ball went straight for the gutter. His crushed expression broke her heart. Then Cole went to stand beside her son—their son—and her heart developed another crack. He put his hand over Robbie's to help steady his arm for his next roll. The ball made its exceedingly erratic way down the lane. In excruciatingly slow motion, eight pins fell. Robbie gave a happy shriek and threw his arms around Cole's waist, and her heart crumbled to bits.

In her turn at the lane, she rolled a strike. All three kids cheered and held their hands in the air. Laughing, she went down the line, giving them double high fives.

Cole had risen to take his turn next. When he raised his palm, she hesitated for only a moment, then high-fived him. He caught her fingers and squeezed lightly.

"The guys brought a ringer in, huh?" he asked. He smiled at her. "*Game on,* lady."

Shaking her head, she went back to her seat.

She hadn't come here tonight to compete with him.

Cole bowled a strike, ran the gauntlet of hands on his way back, and gave her another high five that left her palm warm and tingling. Wanting to hold onto the feeling, she curled her fingers into a fist in her lap.

As he dropped into the seat next to hers again, he draped his arm across the back of her chair. When he had wrapped his arm around her at the Hitching Post, both his touch and his warmth made her want to lean into him…just as she fought against doing now.

After swallowing hard, she said, "At least you're being a good sport."

"Not like I had a choice about all this," he muttered. He made a gesture that took in the kids, the lanes and the Lucky Strike.

When she had come downstairs to meet him tonight, he had been waiting for her in the sitting room. As she entered the room, Rachel and the boys had swarmed past her, roughhousing and ready for a night at the bowling alley, thanks to the discussion she had just had with them in the dining room.

All because she had come to her senses about the idea of a night on the town alone with Cole. Much as she wanted to be with him, she had to think about what was best for Robbie.

Cole sat glowering at her, but his expression didn't fool her. He had paid attention to her all through dinner, smiling at her as he joked with the kids, drawing her into the conversation when she grew quiet, holding such steady eye contact with her at times that they might have been the only two people in the room.

She might have been special to him.

His interest fanned her hopes of finally getting closer to what she'd always dreamed of having. Cole and a family. But she couldn't let herself fall for those hopes or believe in those dreams.

Once again, pride shot through her. "You did ask for *all this*, you know. And you deserve it, for twisting my arm to get me to agree to come out with you." Still, a tiny twinge of guilt ran through her. "But you didn't invite the kids along. I did. I'm happy to pay—"

He leaned closer.

She clutched her hands in her lap.

"You can expect to pay for this, all right." With one finger, he traced a path along her chin, not touching her lips but close enough to make them tingle. "And don't worry about needing your calculator. I won't look for reimbursement in cash."

ON THE RIDE HOME, Tina managed to force half her mind to focus on the kids' chatter and fought with the other half to keep it from straying to Cole.

She gave up altogether on trying to control her body.

From nerves, she had licked her lips so often, they felt dry, leaving her craving another drink of sweet tea. Or a taste of something she might enjoy even more...

Despite the caution she'd given herself, anticipation raced through her. Though they rode the final miles to the ranch along flat, unpaved road, when Cole pulled into the parking area behind the Hitching Post, she felt as if they had just taken a roller-coaster ride.

She glanced over at the back porch. In the kitchen doorway, Jed stood as though he'd been on sentry duty waiting for them to return.

Cole came around to her side of the truck to open her door, just as he had done outside the Bowl-a-Rama. The gesture touched her this time, too.

Then she saw he hadn't backed away.

He stood only an arm's length from her, making it impossible for her to exit the truck without brushing up against him. Well, if he still wanted to play games...

"'Bout time you brought those kids home again," Jed called. "Get in here, you rascals, you're about to miss out on the popcorn."

Cole stepped back.

Ignoring her surge of disappointment, she climbed down and moved aside.

After they left the bowling alley, they had dropped Scott

off at Layne's new apartment. Now Rachel and Robbie tumbled from the backseat of the truck, nearly knocking her over in their dash to the porch.

"Kids," Cole muttered.

"Gotta love 'em," she said.

"Not tonight. I'm off duty as of now, at least until tomorrow."

She heard the relief in his voice. In the space of a day, he spent such limited time with the kids. How would he ever handle being a full-time daddy?

When she moved, intending to pass him, he leaned one shoulder against the truck and crossed his arms, settling in. "Going somewhere?" he murmured.

She looked beyond him toward the hotel. Jed and the kids had gone, leaving the porch empty and the back door securely closed. Long habit must have made Jed turn out the porch light.

They stood in darkness except for the low lamps lining the walkway and the soft glow of a cloud-covered moon.

"Enjoy yourself tonight?" he asked.

"Yes, actually. The kids all had fun. So did I."

"Yeah, I could see being with them was right up your alley."

A nervous giggle escaped her. "That was an awful pun."

"I could stop talking."

She swallowed. "You seemed to enjoy yourself, too. It's a shame you don't get to see Scott more often. You don't know him very well, do you?"

"I'm getting to know all the kids around here now." He shook his head. "But no, I don't know Scott well. After Layne's first divorce, she would come my way for a weekend once in a while. I saw him a few times then, but he was just a baby. Once she remarried, those trips came to an end. Terry tended to keep them close to home."

Close to Cowboy Creek, the hometown Cole had avoided till recently.

"And now he's made her leave their home?" she said.

He shrugged. "Technically, he asked her to move because he's selling the house. The money from that will help her out. Provided he turns over her share. He's not so hot at sticking to his promises," he muttered. "But that's what I'm here for."

"That's what big brothers *are* for," she said, smiling.

"Yeah. Anyhow, she'll manage." He glanced away. "But she might not have the kind of happy ending you like."

She swallowed a sigh. After all these years, he still knew her so well.

"You didn't have a happy ending, either, did you?" She half turned from him and rested back against the truck. "I mean, with what you told me about getting left at the altar. You must still be dealing with the hurt."

He shook his head. "It was a crazy notion, trying to get together when we barely knew each other. No hurt. No harm, no foul. I was only out the price of a ring."

But you did try. How can you say you don't believe in marriage?

Before she could find a way to ask the question, he glanced quickly toward the hotel, then back again.

His eyes shining, he looked down at her and said, "I'd walk you to the door to say good-night, but as I'm staying at the hotel, that's my door over there, too. And I don't know where your room is."

"The family wing." She blurted the words in relief. He wouldn't attempt to walk her to *that* door, not when he knew how that would raise their chances of having an audience. Here, they were alone.

She still didn't know how she felt about that.

One side of his mouth curled, carving a deep dimple

into his cheek, as if he'd read her mind and found her thoughts amusing. "'Family wing?'"

She nodded. "Down the hall, past Jed's den and the kitchen. Jed and Abuela and Robbie all have their rooms down there, too."

He didn't respond.

She toyed with the end of her braid.

He looked down. "In all the years I've known you, I've never seen you without your hair all tied up."

The comment reminded her of Ally, who always urged her to let her hair loose, to wear bright colors. To lighten up and brighten up. To get a life. She reminded her best friend she preferred neutral colors and patterns that didn't stand out. She told Cole now what she always ended up saying to Ally. "I'm a hotel bookkeeper-slash-waitress-slash-whatever-help-is-needed. The hairstyle is practical."

As she lifted her braid, intending to slip it over her shoulder, Cole reached up to touch the woven strands.

Her breath caught in her throat.

Their gazes locked.

For a fleeting moment, they were teenagers in the back of his truck, stealing kisses and on the verge of making love... He had reached for her braid and begun to tug on the elastic at the end of it. Laughing, she had pushed his hands away and managed to distract him...

Now, he gave her a full smile that took her breath away. "I think it's time for us both to stop talking."

He ran his finger down her bare arm, raising a trail of goose bumps. Warning lights flashed in her brain. Too many negatives, too many reasons she shouldn't be with him like this, too many memories proving why she shouldn't let him get any nearer.

Including his claim he would never settle down.

Yet, no matter what he said about not caring he'd been

left at the altar, his attempt proved he hadn't always been against the idea of marriage.

That one thought gave her the strength to hang onto her dreams.

He leaned in, hovering close enough to send warmth from the whole long length of his body to cover her like an afghan. All her logic and reasoning and warnings failed her. Her thoughts disappeared under a rush of pure passion. And her schoolgirl crush gave way to very adult desires.

He ran his fingers up her arms. This time, goose bumps blended with ripples of pleasure until she couldn't tell one from the next. All she knew for certain was that she had waited five years for this.

He cupped her face with his hands, brushed her cheekbones with his thumbs, and finally—*finally*—touched his mouth to hers. More sensations mingled and swept through her. The taste of peppermint candy… The warmth and weight of his mouth… The secret thrill of finding his here-and-now kiss even better than those from her memories.

Much, much better.

Chapter Twelve

"And, so? How did your evening go?"

At the kitchen table, Tina sat watching Abuela prepare her potato casserole for tomorrow's breakfast. The question made her quickly raise her mug to cover her smile. Hot tea stung her lips, still tender from Cole's kisses.

Who knew where the evening would have *continued* to go, if Robbie hadn't run out to remind them Jed had made popcorn. Somehow, she hadn't minded the interruption. Not when Cole had smiled and tousled Robbie's hair. Not when Cole had laughed as her son—*their* son—took them both by the hand to lead them into the house.

"Everything went just fine," she said. "The kids had a great time."

"*Ah*...the kids." The rasp of the potato against the ricer picked up speed. "And...?"

"I enjoyed myself, too."

"I'm sure of that. And Cole?"

"He had a good time, too, I think."

After watching her *abuela* work in this kitchen for so many years, she could follow every movement with her eyes closed.

White shreds flew into the stone bowl Abuela liked because it was large enough to hold all the shredded potatoes, covered with water to keep them overnight. In the morning, she would use her old wooden tortilla press to squeeze the potatoes dry.

Between her need to guard herself against Cole and her desire to be with him, she felt a bit pressed herself.

Abuela smiled. "He would visit me here in this kitchen sometimes, and sit right where you sit now."

"He did?" Her voice rose in astonishment. What else had Abuela never told her? "When was this?"

"When you would do your homework upstairs in your attic room. On Fridays especially. After he came for his pay and sat talking with Jed, he would come and stay in the kitchen for a while. He liked my desserts."

"He still does," she confirmed with a laugh. "You saw him the other night. He almost wrestled Jane over the last serving of your flan. But you never told me about Cole coming into the kitchen."

"Many times, I would make flan on Friday because I knew he would enjoy it." Abuela smiled again. "Something about that boy I always liked."

Her jolt of surprise almost made her spill the tea. "Really? You never told me that, either."

"You didn't need my encouragement, did you? I know why you would run to the barn after school every day."

"Oh." She took another, more cautious sip from her mug. "And you didn't mind?"

Abuela laughed. "Only when you didn't complete your chores."

Tina debated her next question for so long, yet another large potato joined the shreds in the bowl. "Why didn't you say something once you knew how I felt about Cole?"

Now, her *abuela* froze. "I had my secrets," she said at last. "I didn't want to pry into yours."

"And when I got pregnant...did you realize the baby was his?"

"I couldn't know. Not for sure."

"But you suspected?"

"Yes."

"And again, you didn't say anything."

Abuela set the potato and the ricer aside and turned to face her. The lines around her eyes seemed deeper, more pronounced.

Tina held her breath and waited.

After a moment, Abuela crossed the room and took a seat at the table. "From time to time, Cole talked about what he would do with his life and where he would go.

"Thom—your father—always talked about leaving the ranch, too. About leaving Cowboy Creek. And at last, he did. Your mother came to tell me she wanted to follow him. But my Emilia was already pregnant, and I pleaded with her to stay. For her sake and for yours. She listened...for a while." She sighed. "Once you were born, she placed you into my arms, and then she was gone."

Tina's fingers trembled as she reached across the table.

Abuela took her hand and held it tightly. "They were good children, Emilia and Thom, with good hearts, but they were wild. And young. Too young to want to stay here, where they saw no future but a life working on the ranch or at the hotel. A life that Jed and I love. That you now love." Her voice broke.

Tina wanted to go to her, to hold her close, but Abuela reached out to cover their joined hands. "You were never like them, *mi vida*," she said, "but when you told us you were having a baby, I was afraid you would leave Cowboy Creek, too, to search for Cole. And that, like your mother and father, you would never return."

Tina swallowed hard. "I'm not planning to go anywhere. Ever."

"I'll be glad if that stays true. I will be even more glad if you and Cole find happiness."

"It was only one date, Abuela. Please don't get your hopes up." A good reminder for them both.

"I always have high hopes. For you and for Robbie." She sighed. "You know, if I found a way to change the past, I would go back to when you were born and tell Jed the truth."

"If we could change the past, I would tell you and Abuelo, too."

"And Cole?"

She looked down at Abuela's hands, still wrapped firmly around hers. "I had my reasons for not telling him."

"As I had with Jed. But, though Jed didn't know you were his granddaughter, he did know you. He saw you every day. He helped me to raise you. Cole didn't know about Robbie."

Tina said nothing.

"Look at me, *querida*."

She glanced up.

Abuela stared steadily at her. "When I look in your eyes, I see the same hurt I see in Cole's."

TINA GLANCED AROUND her office and shook her head. Her plan to distract herself by overhauling her filing system hadn't worked at all, and now her office was a mess.

With a sigh, she began picking up folders and putting them back into the same file drawers she had taken them from.

Abuela's words kept ringing in her head.

Cole's face kept flashing in front of her eyes.

Her hands stayed busy with the files, but her mind traveled where it wanted. Unfortunately that wasn't very far, just to the parking area outside the Hitching Post.

Cole's good-night kiss had been only a tease, a taste, but it had made her think of the relationship they *could* have had...the relationship she had always longed for.

Yet now she felt more confused than ever. All she knew was she wanted to keep Cole from hurting her son.

When I look in your eyes, I see the same hurt I see in Cole's.

She closed the file drawer. As she turned to pick up another batch of files, she saw Andi standing in the doorway. She and Jane would be leaving after the weekend, and they had gone into town for one last lunch together at SugarPie's.

"Hi. Okay if I come in?"

"Sure. Let me clean off a chair for you." Grateful for the company, she moved a stack of file folders. Talking with Andi would give her something to think about besides her conversation with Abuela.

And besides Cole and his kisses.

Her cousin took a seat and looked around her. "You didn't say anything about renovating your office."

"I'm not renovating. Just doing some filing."

"Oh. Well, Jane and I only got back a few minutes ago." Andi laughed. "I thought I'd never get her away from the dessert tray."

"My best friend gives me the same trouble," she admitted.

"Then you know the feeling. By the way, Sugar and Layne say hello."

"Thanks." She moved more file folders and sat in her desk chair. "Did you and Jane enjoy lunch?"

"Other than dessert, you mean?" Andi smiled. "We did. Layne waited on us. She's putting in extra hours, she said."

"Yes...Cole told me."

"With the new guests in the dining room this morning,

we didn't get to chat much at breakfast. Speaking of Cole, how was your date last night?"

"It was fine." She repeated what she had told Abuela. "The kids had a great time."

Andi smiled. "I guess I don't have to ask if you enjoyed yourself. Your face at breakfast this morning said it all."

Tina stared at her.

"You were...glowing, is how I'd put it."

"That had nothing to do with Cole."

Now Andi laughed. "How do you know I didn't mean bowling with the kids?"

Her cheeks burning, she glanced down at her desk and shifted another pile of folders.

"I hope things work out for you two."

"There's nothing to work out."

"I don't know... Jane and I always saw how you looked whenever you were around Cole. It's the same way you looked this morning. I shouldn't have teased you about him just now, and she shouldn't have teased you the other day. I know you really cared about him." She smiled. "And you never forget your first love."

COLE WIPED THE sweat from his forehead and took a long hard swig of lemonade from his insulated mug.

Paz had provided the lemonade early that morning before he left to meet Pete outside the barn.

"The sun's getting low," Pete said. "Guess we'd better head back."

He nodded. They had started at the farthest point of the fence line they'd scheduled for today and worked their way in the direction of home. But they still had a ride ahead of them.

When he saw the manager was on his cell phone, he climbed into the truck and hoped it wouldn't be a long wait.

It could be Jed or one of the ranch hands who had called, or even Pete's daughter, who had gotten in touch with her daddy a couple of times this afternoon.

He shook his head. Pete had told him she was a talker, and she'd proved that at the bowling alley.

He sat back in his seat, adjusted his Stetson to block the sun from his eyes and tried not to think about that night.

Pete climbed into the truck. "Rachel again," he said, confirming his hunch. "It's been two days, and she hasn't stopped talking about the bowling alley."

"We all had fun," Cole said.

Too much fun, some of us, outside the hotel at the end of that night.

"Well," Pete said, "you've got Rachel's seal of approval, and that's saying something. She doesn't take to folks easily."

"She's a cute kid."

"Your nephew's not bad, either. I saw he looked a little more relaxed yesterday when Tina had him up on Bingo."

"He did, didn't he?"

"You and he seem to be comfortable with each other, too."

He nodded. "We're getting along." Scott had grown more used to him, or maybe it was the other way around.

Robbie seemed just as comfortable.

He couldn't help the feeling of pride that shot through him at the thought.

In the next instant, he glanced away, squinting as he looked out over the horizon. The other day, he hadn't lied when he said he'd felt good about his progress with the kids. But a week or two wouldn't be nearly enough to turn him into the perfect daddy.

A lifetime couldn't help him achieve that.

"Seems to me you're doing fine," Pete said.

The manager sure had more experience than he did. He could learn a lot from him. But he hesitated to ask.

He and Tina hadn't gotten very far with figuring out their plans. His idea of talking things out with her over supper had fallen through the minute she'd walked into the sitting room with the kids.

Since then, several new arrivals had checked into the hotel, including a family with a couple of teenagers. She had spent some time showing them around the hotel and ranch and introducing them to Pete and the wranglers. She'd barely had time for a word with him. Which was probably a good thing.

But even when she was out of sight, he could see her wide, dark eyes beneath arched brown eyebrows, high cheekbones and firm, shapely lips. In the five years since high school, cute, quiet little Tina had blossomed into a real beauty.

Even when he was busy working, he found his mind wandering to her again and again. *Not* a good thing, in any way, shape or form.

And a bad choice of expression, because it only made him think of her in other ways.

They had fit together as though she'd been made for him, with her height putting her at exactly the right place to hold her against his chest, her full curves just the right size and softness for his big hands, her mouth a perfect match to his. And though he hadn't said a word to her about any of this, the way she settled into his arms said she agreed.

If Robbie hadn't come running out to the back porch last night to call them in, who knew what might have happened.

Not getting the chance to find out was probably a good thing, too.

He had a bad feeling he was falling hard for a woman he still didn't trust.

COLE FINISHED STOWING the gear from the ranch truck in the barn, then went outside to try clapping the surface dirt from his clothes.

Jed stood near the corral, his thumbs hooked into his belt loops, watching one of the wranglers leading a teenaged girl around the corral on horseback.

Cole ambled over and reported in on their progress for the day.

Jed nodded. "Sounds good. Everything going along well for you here?"

Cole didn't hesitate with his response. "Fine. It's good to work with Pete again. My nephew's happy to visit. And the food over at the hotel is great."

"Tell Paz that. It'll keep her happy, too."

Cole laughed.

"And the company?" Jed persisted.

"That's fine, too."

The old man had made numerous attempts to increase his interest in the three females at the Hitching Post. Or, that's what he'd thought at first. Over the past few days, he'd begun to suspect it was Tina's name the old man had at the top of his list.

While he didn't intend to get hitched to any of the women—despite that kiss a couple of nights ago—Jed's encouragement came as a relief. If he was pushing his own granddaughters on him, he truly must have forgiven him for walking out years ago.

That knowledge eased some of the burden from his shoulders. The rest, he still had to deal with.

And recently, he seemed to have taken on a whole new load.

That kiss with Tina had turned out a lot more pleasurable than he intended. Thankfully, he'd come to his senses and chalked it up to a nice night out that had helped calm his restless energy. But he hadn't missed the danger signs.

Directly after he'd kissed her, he had read her feelings the way he always had—as easily as he'd read the textbooks in the classes they had shared. Since their night at the bowling alley, he'd seen those feelings in her expression every time he looked her way. It made him glad they hadn't had time alone again.

"You'll be around Saturday night?" Jed asked. "I want you here for the chuckwagon."

"I'll be at Layne's most of the day, doing some painting for her." And a list of other chores.

A run-in with her ex had left her upset, and she'd gotten nothing done around the apartment the night before. The pregnancy was wearing her out, too. Instead of extra hours at SugarPie's, she needed two weeks on a tropical island. But she wouldn't accept that from him, either.

"Once I'm done in town," he added, "I can come back here."

"Good. Jane and Andi both plan to head out the morning after it." Jed sounded sorrowful.

"Yeah, they said. It must've been nice to have them visit, since you hadn't seen them in a while."

Jed nodded. "I miss them every day I don't see them. Don't you feel the same about Layne and her boy?"

"It's different for me."

"The hell it is. Family's family. What made you turn your back on your sister for all these years, Cole?"

"I didn't turn my back. I've always taken care of Layne when she needed me." When she was between husbands.

"Sending money home's not the same as being here, where you belong." His tone sounded accusing.

Maybe the old man hadn't forgiven him, after all. And

why should he? The boss didn't owe him anything. In fact, just the opposite.

"And what about Tina?" Jed demanded.

He froze. After a moment, he forced himself to say evenly, "You know, Jed, since I've been back, I'm fairly sure you've been seeing to it that my path crosses with hers. I appreciate the thought. But you might as well save yourself the trouble. There's not going to be anything between us."

"Can't say that, when you two already have the most important connection of all. Like I said, family's family."

"You mean Robbie." It wasn't a question; he could see the knowledge in Jed's steady gaze. "Well, then, maybe you also know Tina never told me the truth."

"That's Tina's way, too independent for her own good. The girl never told Paz or me, either, till this week."

"So she said. I wasn't sure I believed her."

Jed glared at him. "Maybe that's where you're going off track, son." He sighed. "Now, I intend to keep this conversation between us. And I hope you'll give what I'm going to say some thought. You'll never get anywhere if you don't start taking some things on trust."

That was exactly the problem.

But before Cole could respond, Jed stomped away.

Chapter Thirteen

Hearing Jed's footsteps in the lobby, Tina pushed her notebook away from her on the desk and waited.

Her mind definitely wasn't on her work or even in her office. Instead, her thoughts were with Jed, who had told her he had already begun missing her cousins, though they hadn't even left yet. He also kept returning to her office to fill her in on Jane and Andi's last-minute ideas for the renovations. She didn't know which made her feel worse.

Her thoughts were with Cole, too, though they didn't make her feel much better.

Jed entered the room and settled into the side chair at her desk. "You need to get away from this computer once in a while, girl. Folks will think I never let you leave the office. You're joining us at the chuckwagon tomorrow, aren't you?"

"Of course. You know I wouldn't miss it."

"Good." He exhaled heavily. "It's sure going to be quieter once the girls leave."

"They do add a lot to the conversations," she agreed, smiling.

"Good thing Cole's going to be around, and bringing his nephew by, too. Robbie's tickled to have someone else to play with."

"Yes, he is." Her son had almost become a different

little boy now that he had a constant playmate—one that wasn't a girl. "Rachel's happy about Scott being here, too."

Jed laughed. "Yeah. She especially likes having someone else to boss around. Gotta give Cole a hand, he's doing a good job with all the kids, don't you think?"

She nodded. Even she had to admit, he was diligent about minding Scott for his sister. He was also becoming more and more comfortable in caring for the kids. Beyond that, she could see how much he was beginning to care *about* them.

Then why did he keep insisting he didn't want a family?

"Andi made a point of mentioning what a good job Cole was doing. And Jane had plenty of good things to say about him, too."

"That's great," she said automatically, her thoughts again on the odd coincidence of Cole's return to the ranch now, just when Andi and Jane had come to town again. Before, she hadn't felt she could ask Jed about it. Now she wanted answers.

"I was wondering about this visit," she said.

For a moment, Jed froze. Then he shrugged and settled back in his chair. "I thought it was high time I saw the girls again. I contacted them myself." He sounded defensive—or maybe just hurt that his other granddaughters hadn't taken the first step.

"I'm glad you did," she assured him, "and I know they are, too." She dragged the notebook closer and looked down at it. She was sorry now she had steered the conversation in this direction. Yet she still wanted to know. "I wasn't talking about Andi and Jane. I meant Cole's arrival."

Jed frowned. "What's on your mind?"

"Did you know ahead of time that he was coming back to Cowboy Creek?"

"Nope. Hadn't a clue. Nice that he's back though, isn't it?"

She hesitated, but he sat looking at her. She nodded.

"Now." He slapped his palm on the desk. "Listen to this. I spent some time with the girls this morning, and they came up with a great idea about bringing in a chef."

"A *chef*?"

"Yeah. Andi's going to ask around, talk with some of the folks she knows, maybe find someone who's looking to relocate. Sounds like a good idea to me. The girls said if we're going to put this place on the map, we need to provide top-notch service."

Before she could respond, she heard heavy footsteps on the lobby floor. A moment later, Cole appeared in the office doorway.

"Hey," Jed said, "you two want to chat. Let me get out of the way."

"You're not—" she began.

He brushed her off with a wordless wave. She frowned. Jed left the room, and Cole stepped inside.

"Got a minute?" he asked.

It didn't seem to matter whether she did or not. He took a seat in the leather chair Jed had just vacated and stretched his long legs out in front of him. She would have to step over them to leave.

Speaking of which...

"I don't suppose you're here to check out?"

Now he frowned. "No. What gave you that idea?"

"Wishful thinking, maybe."

"Very funny." He shot a glance toward the empty doorway. "Did Jed say something?"

"No, nothing." Not meeting his eyes, she riffled through the pages of her notebook.

"What's wrong?"

He put his hand over hers. The spark of excitement she felt at his touch should have warned her to pull away. But she didn't think of flashing red lights. She thought only of the many times she had imagined him here in the hotel, living with her and loving her and helping her create the family she'd always wanted.

"I know something's bothering you," he murmured. "Talk to me."

She struggled to remind herself she couldn't fall for this again, couldn't let him turn his charms on her and get away with it. "Why?" she demanded.

He frowned. "I don't know what I've done to get on your bad side. But I think we can change that."

"Why would we want to?"

He laughed. "Dang, woman, you ask more questions than all the kids put together. Come on, we've barely had a chance to talk at all in the past couple of days. Admit it, you've missed me, haven't you?"

"Don't flatter yourself."

"All right, then. How about I flatter you?"

His question sent a burst of pleasure through her. Somehow, she managed to say levelly, "How about you don't? I wouldn't want you wasting your breath."

"All right, then," he said again. "I won't." He leaned forward and touched his mouth to hers.

Now warmth spread all through her, followed by a rush of desire. She had curled her fingers in the fabric of his shirt, ready to draw him closer, when he smiled.

Once, that same slow smile had held the power to break her heart. So had he.

Now the warning lights flashed.

WHEN TINA SAT back against her chair and twined her fingers in her lap, Cole fought not to reach for her again. He slumped back in his own seat and shoved his hands into his jeans pockets.

In the space of a heartbeat he'd gone from wanting to find out what had upset her to wanting a heck of a lot more. When he'd walked in here, that kiss sure hadn't been in his plans.

Time to back off, to steady himself. To find some solid ground. "I interrupted your talk with Jed. It seemed like the conversation wasn't going well."

"It was fine."

He smiled wryly. "It wouldn't hurt to give me credit for *some* brains. Something's up. And I don't think it's got to do with…what just happened here. You'd already looked upset when I came to the doorway."

He had always loved Tina's dark eyes. They looked even more beautiful when they gleamed as they did now. It wasn't till she blinked hard and looked away that he saw she was fighting for composure.

"Hey," he murmured. "Come on, you'll feel better if you talk about it. Are you still worrying about the changes Jed's making to the hotel?"

For a moment, he thought she wouldn't answer.

"It's not just renovations now," she said at last. "Andi and Jane are trying to convince him to hire a chef."

"For the weddings? That makes sense."

"Yes," she said grudgingly. "I'd factored in hiring caterers for any events we book for the banquet room. But Jed's not talking about parties and wedding receptions. He means hiring another chef in the kitchen. Which *doesn't* make sense. No matter how popular the Hitching Post becomes, we've only got so many rooms. Abuela accommodates all the guests with help from just the kitchen staff. And from me, if they take time off unexpectedly. We would never have a need for two full-time cooks."

"Then tell Jed. He's a reasonable man."

"I don't know how reasonable he is, but this is the last

straw." She sighed. "The Hitching Post can't afford all this." She spoke so softly, he had to lean forward again to hear her. "More staff, yes, but not if we implement almost any of the upgrades Andi and Tina have suggested."

"Then don't do them. You said you didn't want to see changes around here, anyway."

Her eyes gleamed again.

He recalled their conversation that day in the sitting room. "This is more than just a hotel to you. You told me that. It's your home."

"It's not just that," she said. "It's Jed. You heard what he said when he announced his plans. This is what he wants. And I owe him too much not to help him achieve his dream."

"Sometimes dreams don't measure up against reality."

She flushed and looked away. "Maybe they don't."

"Jed can always talk to his bank."

She said nothing.

He frowned. "He won't agree to a loan, will he?"

Again, she didn't answer. She wouldn't even look in his direction. He'd bet if he hadn't stretched his legs out in front of him, blocking her way, she would have gotten up and walked out of the room.

Nodding slowly, he said, "That's it. He won't take out a loan. I remember once Jed said he hasn't trusted bankers since his grandfather told him about losing his life's savings in the Depression."

"He keeps enough money in checking to take care of payroll and bills. But he'd never pay interest to a bank."

"Then just explain to Andi and Jane they need to ease up on the spending."

Her eyes flashed. "And what? Tell them they're building their grandfather's dreams on money he doesn't have? Obviously, he doesn't want them to know or he would have said something himself. And just because my job gives me inside knowledge, I can't be the one to tell them."

COLE SPENT MOST of Saturday doing some painting at Layne's apartment while she was at work. Andi and Jane had offered to watch Scott, and he had picked up the boy and dropped him off at the Hitching Post earlier that morning.

When Layne arrived home in midafternoon, he had just finished the last of the trim in the living room. "The paint's already dry in Scott's room. I did that one first and moved the furniture back into place already."

She sank onto the couch and put her feet up. "I don't know how I'm ever going to thank you for all this." She touched her stomach. "I could name the baby after you."

He laughed. "What if it's a girl?"

"I'll call her Colette. Or Colleen."

"I think you'd better come up with something else, even for a boy. I'm one of a kind, you know."

"That *is* true."

Frowning, he set the paint tray on the plastic tarp and settled on the short step stool.

"What?"

He shrugged. "I'm helping you pick out your baby's name. I didn't get to do that for my own."

"You missed out on a lot," she said softly. "But you're catching up now. How's Robbie?"

"Good. He and Scott are like twins."

"Scott's so happy to have a new friend. I'm thrilled our kids are cousins. And how are you and Tina getting along?"

He picked up the paint tray and rose from the stool. "It's complicated."

"Most relationships are."

"So is being a parent."

"You've got that right. And when the kids are as little

as our guys, it's hard to get a handle on things. They grow so fast. They change so much. No two days—no two conversations—are the same. And speaking of conversations," she said lightly, "don't think I didn't notice how you redirected this one."

"I didn't redirect. There's not a lot going on with the two of us."

"Just what I like. A man who doesn't kiss and tell."

He almost lost his grip on the paint tray. Hoping to cover his startled reaction, he leaned down to pick up the can of paint he had left beside the ladder.

When he finally looked at Layne again, he found her grinning at him.

"Not a lot going on, huh?"

"Nothing worth talking about yet."

"*Yet?* That's good. At least you're staying open to possibilities."

But I shouldn't be.

Relieved to get out of the room, he carried the paint tray into the bathroom to clean the brushes.

He shouldn't think about Tina, either, but he couldn't get her out of his mind.

When he had kissed her that night after their date and then again in her office, he had made the mistake of looking into those dark eyes he had always felt drawn to. In them he read more than he wanted to know. He saw what he had realized as a teen all those years ago and what had made him want to back off, then and now.

She wanted a relationship. Something lasting. Something permanent.

All things he didn't do.

BY THE TIME Cole got back to Garland Ranch, Pete and the other wranglers had the campfire blazing. From the parking area, he could see smoke rising and hear the sound of faraway voices.

He thought of Tina's voice and what she had said before he'd left her that afternoon. Long after their conversation had ended, her words seemed to echo inside his head.

I owe him too much not to help him achieve his dreams...

He owed the old man a huge debt, too.

He'd put into motion the one thing he could do that might help him finally write that debt off. Before he had left Layne's, he'd called the friends he had talked with a while back about pooling some cash for a good investment. Those friends might be his answer to the question of how to help Jed. At the same time, he could solve Tina's financial dilemma.

To tell the truth, he didn't know which would give him the most satisfaction.

The kitchen door of the hotel swung open. Tina stepped onto the porch. A loaded serving tray rested on her upturned forearm. In her other hand, she clutched several paper sacks she seemed in danger of dropping.

He hurried across to the porch and vaulted the steps to take the sacks from her hand.

She exhaled heavily and leaned against the railing. "Thanks. Those were all more awkward to carry than I'd expected. Did you get much accomplished at Layne's?"

"Making progress. She ought to be settled in soon." He hefted the sacks. "Looks like I arrived in the nick of time."

"We could have used you even more an hour ago."

"Why? Something wrong?"

"Scott had a meltdown when Pete told him he couldn't help build the fire."

He winced. "Sorry to let you in for that. I guess I shouldn't have taken Andi up on the offer and left him here all day. But I've got to be honest and say I've only seen him have one short spat with Rachel. I've never witnessed a full-blown tantrum and probably wouldn't have been much help, anyway."

Still, he couldn't help feeling good that Tina thought he could've handled Scott. Maybe that proved he *had* made some progress in the time he'd been back in Cowboy Creek.

She shrugged. "He calmed down when I told him he could be in charge of giving everyone their bottles of pop."

"Plastic bottles." He nodded. "Good thinking. When it comes to the kids, you beat me hands down."

Her cheeks turned a dusky pink.

He reached up and tapped her chin lightly just below those soft, pink lips he wanted to taste again. But not here in the afternoon sunshine on the Hitching Post's back porch. Not where someone could come along any moment and see them. Or worse, to interrupt.

"I'd like to think that blush comes from standing so close to me," he said. "But I've got a hunch the compliment's having more of an effect."

Now her entire face flamed.

He transferred one of the sacks to his free hand for safety's sake. His own safety. That platter she held sure didn't create enough space between them. Having his hands full just might keep him from reaching out to her again.

"No need to feel embarrassed," he said. "I'm only stating the truth."

"You don't need to compliment me for it. I'm just doing the best I can, like everyone else does."

"Not everyone," he said grimly. "Some folks haven't got what it takes to be a parent." He tried to push away the memory of his father's face. "But you're a heck of a mom. And you've done a great job with Robbie."

She pressed her lips together, forcing their softness

into a firm line. The sight piled yet more guilt onto him, a weight he couldn't shift the way he could the sacks in his hands.

She shrugged. "I've had help."

"But not from me," he said shortly.

"I didn't say that."

"You didn't have to. I see it in your face."

"You're so sure you know everything that crosses my mind, aren't you?"

"Yeah, I am. You're easy to read. You always have been."

"Maybe," she agreed. "Or maybe I've always let you read only what I want you to know." Brushing past him, she went down the stairs.

Yeah. And maybe you've always told me only what you want me to know.

Lies of omission are still lies.

Either of those thoughts were enough to make him keep his distance. Yet he was finding it more and more difficult to stay away.

Chapter Fourteen

Her seat in the shadows on the far side of the fire ring, away from the crowd, allowed Tina a full view of the entire campsite. Automatically, she scanned the area for anything that might spoil the evening for their guests. Technically, Pete and the cowhands oversaw all the dude ranch activities. But even as a child, she had considered herself their backup. Part of the team.

Her scan complete, she looked across the fire ring at her son.

Robbie sat beside Cole, who at this very moment was breaking her heart. When he had claimed some people didn't know what it took to be a parent, she knew he had meant himself. And yet he had spent most of this evening with Robbie and Scott, doing exactly what a parent did best.

Days ago, she had noticed how Scott had taken to her son. Now Robbie seemed to have done the same with Cole. He had shadowed him all evening, dogging his heels and doing everything Cole did.

Cole had chosen Robbie as his teammate for a game of horseshoes. The last horseshoe clanged, hitting its mark. Cole high-fived Robbie. They had won.

She couldn't keep from cheering along with the rest of the crowd.

Cole smiled at her across the open space between them, and her heart gave a tiny leap, just the way it had every time he had looked her way in school.

"Got any room left on that log?"

Startled, Tina turned to see Jane standing beside her. She scooted sideways. "Have a seat."

Jane sank gracefully onto the log. She wore jeans and a T-shirt in her usual black. Though Tina found the color even blander than her own neutral choices, she had to admit black suited the other woman, making her look taller and slimmer and more sophisticated than ever.

"Not a bad view from here." Jane looked across the fire ring. At Cole.

"There are some extra seats over there."

"Hey," Jane said. "Showing your claws, aren't you, cuz?"

To her dismay, her cheeks burned just as they had when she'd stood on the porch with Cole, only not for the same reason. Jane hadn't given her a compliment. Still, her tone hadn't sounded malicious, and she sat smiling.

"Sorry," Tina said. "I didn't mean that the way it must have sounded. I just thought you might like getting closer and need a push."

"Closer to Cole? I don't think so. He's all yours."

"No, he's not."

"You could have fooled me."

She stiffened. Abuela had admitted knowing all along about her schoolgirl crush on Cole. Andi had said something similar. A week ago, she wouldn't have followed up on Jane's comment. "What do you mean?"

"You watch him... He watches you... That's what I mean."

"We're just keeping an eye on the kids."

"Yeah, right." Jane laughed softly, her teeth flashing.

Everything about her gleamed in the firelight—her eyes, her dark, shoulder-length hair, the silver jewelry she favored. She shook her head and tapped the camera hanging by its strap from her neck. "You'll be surprised when I show you a couple of the shots of you and Cole together."

"You might as well delete them."

"And you might regret that."

What did it matter? She had plenty of regrets. She wrapped her arms around her knees and stared at the flames.

"You don't want the photos now," Jane added softly, "but you might want them in the future. For Robbie."

Tina froze. "How—?"

"How do I know? I notice similarities."

"And when did you notice these?"

"As soon as I got here."

Now she turned to meet Jane's eyes. "Who else knows?"

"No one. Not from me, anyhow. And Andi hasn't said anything. I doubt she picked up on it." She glanced quickly across the fire ring and back at Tina. "Except for their eyes, the likeness isn't that obvious. It's just apparent to me because I spend a lot of my time behind the camera, watching faces."

For a moment, Jane looked as upset as she felt.

"I'd appreciate it," Tina said, "if you'd keep this conversation to yourself."

"Don't worry. I intend to." Suddenly, she smiled. "But the night's still young. You might feel differently about that even before I board the plane back to New York tomorrow."

Tina hesitated, on the verge of telling Jane that since Cole had returned, she didn't seem able to understand her feelings at all.

Before she could say anything, Jane rose. "I think I'll go make another one of those s'mores."

After she walked away, Tina stole a glance across the fire ring.

Cole had kicked back with a beer, and the boys had done the same with bottles of pop. Cole guzzled his last few mouthfuls and then pretended to make a basket as he dropped the empty bottle in the tall metal bin. He lifted first Robbie, then Scott so they could make their shots too.

Years ago, she'd had so many good reasons for not telling him about her pregnancy. He had dumped her. He was nothing but a playboy. He had left Cowboy Creek and his sister and everyone else behind him and never came back. She had struggled to hang on to all those reasons by reinforcing them with the most important fact of all. The reason she couldn't share her secret.

Cole could never be a good daddy to her son.

But now he had returned and she had seen him with Robbie and Rachel and the boys, she realized she had been deceiving herself.

Yes, he sometimes was apprehensive around the kids. But he was also always patient and attentive and kind.

She thought of what he had said about getting left at the altar, about not wanting to get married, not wanting a family of his own.

Maybe he had been deceiving himself, too.

LATER IN THE EVENING, one of the cowhands brought out a guitar. The guests clustered around, eager to join in a singalong.

Cole had been vigilant about watching the boys while they roasted their franks over the campfire. He didn't feel paranoid about it, but neither did he want to think about what could have happened if he hadn't kept his eyes open. One moment of inattention… One distraction that lasted too long…

Taking care of kids was a full-time job. Being a responsible parent meant working 24/7. Any fool could see that.

Being the best daddy a man could be...

He had no frame of reference for that one. But the more time he spent with Robbie, the more it worried him.

Robbie sat rubbing his cheeks.

"Tired?" he asked.

"Huh-uh. But that smoke keeps getting in my eyes."

"All right, then. Let's head this way. I think it's time for dessert now, anyway." Cole led the boys upwind and watched them run to join Andi and Jane near the picnic table still laden with food.

Their relocation brought them within a few yards of Tina, who had been sitting on the fringes of the action for most of the evening. He sauntered across the clearing and took a seat on the log beside her. "Just thought I'd mosey on over and stake a claim before this spot gets taken."

She smiled and slipped her braid behind her shoulder. "You noticed Jane sitting here earlier."

"No. I noticed you."

She shifted as if she felt uncomfortable. When her hip bumped against his, he damned sure felt something, too, but uncomfortable wasn't it. "Same old Tina, always shying away when someone tries to give you a compliment."

"I'd say calling someone 'same' and 'old' cancels out the compliment."

He laughed. "That's not what I meant, and you know it."

"People don't always say what they mean. And sometimes they don't mean what they *do* say."

"That's a little deep for me. Maybe it's the couple of beers I had after the horseshoes."

"I don't think so. You're smarter than you let on. I should know."

He laughed again, more softly. "Yeah. Which reminds

me, I never did thank you for English and biology. I won't say I'd have flunked those classes in senior year, but you sure helped keep my grade point average from crashing."

"You're welcome. And I never thanked you for..."

"For what?"

She took a deep breath and let it out again. "This wouldn't be the place to discuss it."

The place and the time might never be right for some conversations.

He thought about what she had said to him earlier.

Maybe I've always let you read only what I want you to know.

He didn't like the statement then and he liked it even less now. He also didn't like her blank expression or the feeling of her shutting him out.

"Speaking of high school..." He rubbed his hand across the back of his neck and said sheepishly, "I probably acted like an ass a lot back then."

"'Probably acted like?' Mr. Franklin would have given you a solid D for a sentence like that one."

He shot a glance at her. Quiet little Tina didn't look at him, but he saw the tiny smile curving the corners of her full lips. "All right, then. I behaved like an utter jackass. Is that better?"

"It's a start."

"Anything else I need to brush up on besides grammar?"

She wrapped her arms around her knees and stared at the fire. "You could practice your storytelling skills," she said finally. "You could tell me why you left Cowboy Creek."

Now he took a turn staring off somewhere else.

Near the picnic table, Jane and the boys were skewering marshmallows. The fire still crackled. The singalong had mellowed to a ballad. One of the couples staying at the hotel waved as they walked past. He nodded back, then linked his fingers together and stared down at them.

He could never give Tina what she wanted, could never offer her a future together. But that didn't mean he shouldn't make up for the past. Or try to. He owed her an apology just as much as he owed his debt to Jed.

"This is going to take some time," he said. "To give you an explanation, I have to go back to a while before I left town."

"I think we've got the time."

She glanced over at the boys and evidently considered them in good hands, because she settled herself more comfortably on the log beside him. Again, her hip brushed his, and again, he felt a lot of things…

No, he'd go for an A grade on this one.

He felt a spark as hot as the blazing fire and a damned foolish desire to tell Tina anything she wanted to know.

"Want another header on that?"

Cole placed his hand over his coffee mug and shook his head. He and Jed were alone in the hotel kitchen. "No, I think I've had enough. As it is, I'll be up half the night."

Up and stimulated from caffeine and restless energy and thoughts of bumping hips with Tina.

He hadn't told his story, after all. Robbie and Scott had come over, wanting to go back home. While she and the other women had brought the kids back here to the hotel, he and Jed had stayed to help the cowhands douse the fire and clean up the campsite. Then they'd taken a slow ride home in one of the ranch's SUVs.

"You won't be the only one awake," Jed said.

"You, too, huh?"

He laughed. "No, I sleep like a log."

The word *log* made him think again of sitting beside Tina. He shifted in his seat.

Jed turned off the teakettle on the back burner and poured water into a mug beside the stove.

Cole frowned. "You mean the boys are still up?" That morning, Layne had given the okay for Scott to stay overnight. The three boys, armed with Robbie's sleeping bag and some extra blankets, had taken over Andi's hotel room floor.

"The kids are okay. I checked in with Andi when we got back. I meant Tina."

He recalled what she had told him about having her room in the family wing off the kitchen. His ears had been half tuned for her footsteps since they'd returned to the hotel, but he hadn't heard a thing. "I thought she and Paz had gone to bed already."

"Paz, yeah, she's not much of a night owl. Not like Tina. The light was on in the attic when we drove in, and she hasn't passed by here. That means she's in her room up there, probably with her nose in a book."

"She's still a big reader?"

"When she has some spare time to sit in one place. We keep her moving around here. I don't know what I'd do without that girl."

"Yeah. This project for the hotel has her hopping, doesn't it?"

Jed nodded. "Sure does." He began puttering around the kitchen.

Cole took another mouthful of coffee. It was too soon to say anything to Jed about his plan to offer financial assistance for the renovation, but he ought to have the deal firmed up soon.

He hadn't had the opportunity to mention it to Tina.

He had more important things to talk to her about.

"Well, I think I'm turning in," Jed said. "Want to do an old man a favor and save him another trip upstairs?"

"Sure. I'm headed up there, anyway. Do you want me to look in on the kids?"

"Nah, they'll be fine. Andi knows where to find us if she needs us." He held up the insulated mug, now covered with a lid. "I usually run this up to Tina when I know she's going to be reading late. But I'll tell you, I don't think my legs can make it. Playing horseshoes tonight wore me out. You could drop this off with her."

Cole hesitated, then shrugged. "Sure." He got up to rinse his coffee mug and leave it in the sink.

Jed turned off the light, and they parted ways in the hallway. The old man shambled toward the family wing.

Cole watched him go. Jed had been doing a masterful job of pushing Tina at him.

How would she feel about Jed trying to get them together, if she knew about it? Would she go for the idea?

More likely, it would have been another item on her list of worries. Though the thought bothered him, it might also explain why he had been dragging his heels about conversations they should be having. He didn't want to add to her stress.

He wished he hadn't been a jackass in high school.

And for the first time in his life, he wondered whether he should have stayed in Cowboy Creek all along.

Chapter Fifteen

As Tina turned another page in the book she hadn't been able to focus on, she heard boot steps on the stairs leading up to her attic room. They weren't Jed's slow, measured steps but another lighter tread that had become just as familiar to her.

As she rested the book in her lap and focused on the open door, her heart suddenly felt a bit lighter, too.

Cole came to a stop in the doorway.

"Well, hello," she said in a hushed voice. She rose from the couch. "Are you lost?"

"Almost. You sure didn't bother to leave any bread crumbs." His voice, lowered, too, sounded deeper and even sexier than usual.

When he lifted her tea mug, she smiled and crossed the room to take it from him. "Jed?"

"Yeah. He said this has become part of his nightly ritual when he knows you're up here."

"He's too good to me."

"From what I've seen, you're good to him, too."

"Thanks."

"Well, I'll see you tomorrow." He began to turn away.

She held the mug in both hands, cradling its slight warmth against her, as if it could banish the chill she felt at the thought of his leaving. "Cole."

He stopped and looked back at her.

At the campsite, the boys had run up to them just as he had been close to confiding why he had left town. "You never told me your story earlier. Now would be a good time."

"Now?"

"Well...yes. If you don't have anything else planned."

He didn't move, and she could see the indecision in his face. His gaze went to the doorway, and for an agonizing moment she thought he would go without answering.

Then he looked past her into the room.

Odd. She hadn't cared a bit what Andi and Jane saw when they looked at her accumulated jumble of furniture and books and knickknacks and school mementos. She had wanted only to get her cousins out of her private room.

Now, though, she felt intensely interested in knowing what Cole thought of everything. And she wanted him in her sanctuary, becoming a part of it, sharing her space.

Hadn't she always wanted that?

He stepped into the room, and she suddenly had the irrational feeling she couldn't breathe because he had taken up *all* the extra space. And maybe the oxygen, too.

Very irrational.

He gestured toward the door. "If we're going to talk, we should close this."

"We should."

She led the way back to the couch, where she curled her feet beneath her and took a bracing sip of hot tea.

Cole wandered around the room, looking from the upholstered couch on one wall to the floor-to-ceiling bookcases on the other and the glass-topped coffee table in between. He stopped here and there to inspect her accounting textbooks and the curio cabinet with her collection of porcelain butterflies.

When he came to take a seat beside her, he looked her over from head to toe. "You're an interesting mix," he said. "Brains and beauty."

"Are you going for the playboy role again?" she asked, fighting the pang of disappointment shooting through her. "If so, please don't bother. But I thought you had a story to tell."

He picked up the novel she had left on the couch and riffled through the pages. "I do, but it may not be as interesting as your book."

"Try me."

She listened, not moving a muscle except to take a sip of tea from time to time, as he told her about what had happened five years ago. About his father dying and then his mom following not long after, and about his struggle—while he was still a teen himself—to provide for his younger sister.

To her, the simply told story was more heart-wrenching than any book she had in this room.

Then he told her about needing money for Layne's birthday gift and, more important, to buy groceries for them both.

Her breath caught as she thought about how hard it must have been for him. And for Layne.

"That first day I came back to the hotel, when Jed and I went to talk in his den, I reminded him how he had advanced my pay. Twice. And he wanted to know why I hadn't asked again." After a long pause, he said, "I couldn't ask him for more money. I already felt I'd let him and Layne down, that I should have done a better job managing what I had." He gave her a lopsided smile. "I never was the math whiz you are."

"And I never had parents or brothers and sisters, but I always had Abuela and Jed. Living here in the hotel, I've never in my life gone hungry. You did what you thought you had to do, the best way you could."

His eyes gleamed. He reached up to touch her cheek. "Sweet Tina. I should have known you wouldn't judge. I didn't like borrowing, but yeah, at the time I couldn't think of an alternative."

"I'm sure Jed's forgiven you. He doesn't hold a grudge. But...you still haven't told me why you left."

He shrugged. "I'd always planned to get out of Cowboy Creek. Soon after our mama died, Layne wanted to marry her boyfriend. She wasn't old enough yet, but since I was her legal guardian, I had the right to approve or refuse to sign the papers." Not meeting her eyes, he riffled through the pages of her book again. "She begged and begged, and I didn't know what the hell to do. I wanted to see her happy. So even though she intended to marry the guy who had just broken her heart, I gave the okay. I thought it was the right decision. And it opened the jail cell door and set me free. But just a few months later, she was pregnant and divorced."

He sounded so devastated, her own heart broke for him. She put her hand on his arm. "It was the right thing for her, at the time."

"Not the way things turned out."

"You couldn't know that."

"Maybe not."

He gave her another lopsided smile, then covered her hand with his. Surprise and pleasure made her tighten her fingers on his arm.

"I've never told anyone that story before."

"I'm glad I'm the first."

"I didn't mean to go on for so long."

"I'm glad for that, too. I wasn't doing anything up here except reading."

"And how's the book?"

She laughed lightly. "Not as interesting as talking to you." *Or other things we could be doing.* She felt her cheeks flame.

She knew he saw the color in her face and had more than likely read her mind. Smiling, he lifted her hand and kissed the backs of her fingers, his mouth warm against her skin. When he looked up, his face was close to hers, his eyes shining from the reflected glow of her reading lamp.

She held her breath, waiting.

"Being shy, quiet Tina again?" he asked.

"Thinking to heck with shy and quiet." It had never gotten her what she wanted before. She leaned forward to kiss him chastely.

He slipped his arms around her and held her close. "That was a surprise."

"You handled it well."

"Let's see how *you* do."

But his kiss was nothing like hers. In seconds, it went from chaste to enticing and his hands went from her waist to her hips.

She pressed her mouth more firmly against his and threaded her fingers through his hair.

"My turn?" he asked, running his hand down the length of her braid.

She nodded, suddenly nervous but not willing to back down. Ready to say to heck with everything.

For a moment, he fumbled with the elastic tie. She watched his eyes gleam and his lips curve into a smile as he unraveled the braid until her hair hung loose and flowing around her. He ran his fingers down the wavy lengths, letting his fingertips skim her body, making her shiver.

She had always wondered how she would feel if she let him touch her like this.

And now she knew.

Like this made her feel pleasured and possessed and more excited than she had ever imagined.

Like this reinforced what she had always known.

She loved him.

And they belonged together.

AT THE DRESSER in his room, Cole ran his comb through his wet hair.

Suddenly, he envisioned himself sliding his palms down Tina's never-ending waves. Shaking his head, he yanked the towel from around his waist and tossed it onto the bed.

Damn.

So much for the cold shower, his second since last night.

Just thinking about her had him hard all over again… and he hadn't gone beyond anything besides hot kisses, soft curves and touching that unbelievably sexy curtain of hair.

He swore under his breath and thanked his lucky stars he'd found the restraint to get up from her couch. But he hadn't rushed away.

Remembering how he had treated her in high school, he took his time saying his farewells. He had stood with her at the door for a while as they talked, their voices hushed. Had left her smiling as he walked away.

He hadn't had any other option.

He wasn't a high-school kid pushed to the breaking point and desperate enough to make unwise choices.

No matter how much he wanted Tina, giving in to lust for a temporary fling would only lead to regrets for them both. He would be doing her a favor by keeping his distance.

A knock sounded on his door. He looked at the clock near the bed. Five a.m. on a Sunday. If he hadn't needed the cold shower, he wouldn't have been up yet, since he didn't have to go to work. So who would come to his room at this hour?

It could be Andi having trouble with Scott. Or Jed needing help with an emergency on the ranch.

"Be right there," he called.

He retrieved the towel and knotted it around his hips. As he strode to the door, he slid his arms into last night's shirt. He would be presentable enough while he found out who had knocked and what they needed from him.

To his surprise, Tina stood in the dimly lit hallway. "You're awake early," he said warily.

"Not really. I'm usually helping in the kitchen around this time." Her gaze drifted downward, then bounced back up to his face again. "Mind if I chat with you for a minute?"

He hesitated, then stepped back. "If you don't think you'll be compromising yourself, come on in."

"Maybe I'd like to be compromised," she said with a laugh.

"I meant if someone found you here." Frowning, he closed the door behind her. "You've changed."

"So have you. Five years ago, I don't think you'd have thought twice about what would compromise a woman."

"Maybe you're right."

She perched on the foot of his rumpled bed. It wouldn't take much for him to cross the room and tumble her back against the covers.

Instantly, his body reacted to the image. He clutched his fresh shirt in front of him firmly enough to create permanent wrinkles in the fabric. "Well." He cleared his throat. "Everything okay? Something going on with the kids? Or Jed?"

"No, everybody's fine."

"Good." *Then why are you in my room at five in the morning?*

And did he want to know?

Reminding himself he had made up his mind to keep his distance, he turned to the dresser. He stripped off the old shirt and replaced it with the fresh one. As he stood adjusting the collar, her eyes met his in the dresser mirror.

She smiled. "I thought it would be nice if we offered to take Andi and Jane to the airport."

"We?"

She nodded. "We could borrow Pete's van. It's big enough to fit everyone and handle the car seats. And then on the way back, we could stop for breakfast."

We.

"Thanks, but I need to get over to Layne's."

"Oh. Then…dinner out tonight? Just the two of us—finally." She smiled again.

"I don't think that will work, either. Too much to do at the apartment." He grabbed a comb to run through his hair. In the mirror, he saw her reflection. Her eyes were cast down, her expression thoughtful.

"So…" she said. "Last night, you *were* just taking on the playboy role again."

He turned to face her. "No," he said, measuring his words, "I was not."

Eyes narrowed, she tilted her head to look at him.

"What?" he asked.

"I'm just trying to figure things out, since I don't think you and I are on the same page as we were last night. Or even in the same book."

"We're not in a story at all. This is real life, and I'm trying to do the right thing and act like a responsible adult." He shoved his hand through his hair. "Look, I meant what

I said at the campsite. I was a real jackass to treat you the way I did in school, and I'm sorry about that."

"And…what happened last night… Was I supposed to take that as the rest of your apology?"

He swallowed a groan. *That kiss.*

Granted, she had started it, but he'd taken over from there. He hadn't expected the kiss to turn so hot so quickly. Or for their brief time together to have as much impact as it had—on them both.

"Not an apology," he said. "I didn't intend for any of that to happen. Things got out of hand. It was just a few kisses. Damned fine kisses, but that's all. I didn't mean for you to take it as anything more."

He should have known she would, though. He should have been prepared for her to react exactly the way she had this morning.

Hell, he'd have done best to recall the warning he'd given himself about getting too close.

"Tina." He shook his head and tossed the comb onto the dresser. "As nice as last night was, there's no sense in either of us looking for a repeat. I told you, I'm a rolling stone. And you've always been a stay-in-one place, forever kinda girl."

"A forever I always envisioned with you."

He froze. She said nothing else. After a while, he shook his head. "There's nothing I can say to that. I'm not the kind of man to make empty promises. Or any promises at all."

Chapter Sixteen

Tina handed Robbie a paper place mat and a small box of crayons, courtesy of SugarPie's.

Instead of Cole's company on the ride to the airport, she'd had her son along. And Jed, who had decided at the last minute that he wanted to see his family off.

Though she loved having both of them with her, she regretted the trip hadn't gone the way she had originally hoped it would. Neither had her conversation with Cole this morning. The thought of it made her cheeks flush with heat. From between the salt-and-pepper shakers and the sugar dispenser, she plucked a small hand-printed menu she already knew by heart.

"I can have muffins?" Robbie asked. "Grandpa, you promised."

At her son's words, Tina raised the menu higher and blinked hard a couple of times.

I'm not the kind of man to make empty promises. Or any promises at all.

She had to give Cole credit for owning up to that.

And he was right about her. She *was* a forever kind of girl. A happy, stay-at-home accountant. Not the woman she had tried to be last night.

"Of course, you can have muffins," Jed said. "That's why we came to SugarPie's."

Tina nodded, glad to hear the lightness in his tone.

He had sat quietly in the van on the way back to town, his expression glum. Now perched in a pink-cushioned chair in the sandwich shop, he looked much more energetic. That made sense. It had been his idea to stop here on the way back from the airport—a request enthusiastically seconded by Robbie, who loved Sugar's mini-chocolate-chip muffins.

A waitress in a pink uniform and white apron approached their table. Cole's sister. They resembled each other, though his blue eyes didn't have dark circles under them the way hers did.

The thought made her recall what Jane had said about the likeness between Cole and Robbie. Layne could never have seen the similarities, or she would have said something.

"Good morning." Layne looked at Jed. "You're here early."

Tina glanced at her watch and frowned. It was nearly ten thirty, a late brunch by Cowboy Creek standards. Even on the weekends, when folks didn't have to accommodate those with day jobs, all new gossip was shared by eight forty-five.

Across from her at the table, Robbie looked up. Grinning widely, he grabbed his place mat and waved it in the air. "Hey, we're over here!"

She turned to see Scott rushing toward them. Cole stood in the bakery doorway. His too-carefully-blank expression as he stared at their table said he hadn't expected to see them.

Robbie handed Scott a couple of his crayons. "I keep secrets good, right, Grandpa?"

"You sure do, fella."

Jed shot her a look so quick she almost missed it under

her pretense of studying the menu. He turned to Layne. "I wasn't sure how bad traffic would be on the way back to town. We made good time with Tina driving."

"We went fast," Robbie said. "Like my car. *Vroom-vroom*."

Both boys scooted their crayons across the tabletop.

Layne laughed. "You're some driver, Robbie."

She watched him for only a moment, but long enough for Tina to wonder what Cole might have said to her. At some point, she and Layne would have to talk, too.

"Well," Layne added. "I'll give you all a few minutes to decide on breakfast." She walked over to Cole.

Recalling what Robbie had said, Tina leaned across the table and hissed, "'Secrets,' Grandpa?"

"Breakfast at SugarPie's," he said with a grin as wide as her son's had been.

Sugar carried over an extra chair and set it beside Tina. "Here you are, folks. Jed, good seeing you this morning." The grins must have been contagious, because the two of them smiled widely at each other.

As they chatted, Tina watched the boys and held back a sigh.

This morning, the thought of a ride to the airport with Cole had sounded wonderful—but that was *before* their conversation in his room. Now all she wanted was to keep her distance from him.

Unfortunately, he had just taken the chair beside hers.

"Morning," he said, as if it were the first time they had seen each other that day.

He wore a pair of form-fitting jeans and the same shirt she had watched him change into while she had sat on his bed. The fabric looked crisp, smelled fresh and didn't do a thing to take her mind off what lay beneath it.

When he had opened his door, her first sight of him had left her tongue-tied.

She'd had enough trouble trying to focus on their conversation as he walked around the room. His shirt hung open, giving her tantalizing peeks at the same broad chest and taut abs she had braced her hands against last night.

Then, there had been that towel wrapped around his hips. Granted, it was a nice, big, thick hotel towel... But she hadn't needed the added worry of wondering if it would fall free. Or the concern over what she would do if it did.

"See anything you like?" he asked.

Startled at being caught ogling him again—right in the middle of SugarPie's—she looked up at him. Was that a glimmer of amusement in his eyes?

But he simply pointed to the menu in her hands. He was helping her save face. Doing the right thing. Being a responsible adult.

And giving her a subtle reminder of his warning. There would be no repeat of last night.

Cole toyed with breakfast or brunch or whatever Jed would call it. Later on, he'd have a bone to pick with the old man over this. When Jed had mentioned meeting up at SugarPie's, he hadn't said a word about inviting Tina along.

Pushing aside the last bite of his strawberry pancake, he reached for his coffee mug and tried not to think of Tina, seated beside him. That was an almost impossible challenge. She'd tied her hair up again in her prim and proper braid, but all he could envision was the long strands hanging loose around her shoulders.

He tried not to look at her, either, but found that completely impossible. His eyes went to the soft mouth he'd had beneath his last night. A drop of maple syrup dotted her lower lip. He'd give next month's pay for the chance to lick it off.

As if she knew what he'd been thinking, she grabbed a napkin and dabbed at her mouth.

He shifted in his seat, searching for a distraction, and saw the bill Layne had propped against the napkin holder. He reached for it, but Jed snagged it first. For an old man, he had danged good reflexes.

"My treat," Jed told him, tucking the bill beside his plate.

He didn't like the idea but knew he couldn't argue with the man in public. He nodded his thanks and picked up his coffee mug instead. Soon, he might be able to pay his debt back to Jed in full.

At Layne's this morning, he had spent most of his time with his eyes on Scott and one ear glued to the phone. He'd had takers for his idea of investing in the Hitching Post. In a conference call, they had firmed up enough details for him to present their offer to Jed.

The old man rose and pulled his wallet from his hip pocket. "Are you heading back to the ranch, Cole? With the girls gone and our guests checked out, we're gonna need some extra voices to break up the quiet."

Beside him, Tina seemed to sit frozen in place, as if she didn't want to miss his response. Or didn't want to hear it.

"Not right away," he said. "I'm hanging around town for a while. Layne's working till noon, then we've got some things to take care of over at the apartment."

Jed nodded. "Well, you know your room will be waiting."

His room.

He thought about what it would be like to have a permanent place at the Hitching Post. A room he shared with Tina.

Jed headed toward the cash register.

Tina took her purse from where she'd left it hanging from her chair. "I'll be back in just a few minutes," she said. "I'm sure you'll be fine with the kids."

Not sure he could trust his voice, he nodded, avoided looking at her and tried to chase away the visions Jed's words had triggered in his mind.

She rose from her seat.

Across from him, both boys sat working with their crayons. He leaned forward to inspect the place mats. Scott had drawn a picture of what looked like a cat with green fur and orange eyes. "Nice job," he said. He looked at Robbie's picture. "That one's good, too."

"You know what I drawed?"

Tina paused beside him.

Robbie might have been a year older than Scott, but he didn't have much more skill at artwork. Cole couldn't make heads or tails of the bright blotches Robbie had run into each other on the page. But from the way the kid looked at him with his eyes squinted and his forehead wrinkled, Cole could tell a lot was riding on this answer.

"Well," he said, buying time, "I know I've seen one of these before. Maybe even a couple."

Robbie continued to frown.

Silence stretched on.

He imagined a future of searching for and never finding the right answers for his son. Or worse, of saying things he never should say, the way his father had done.

Beside him, Tina moved, breaking him free from his trance.

She leaned forward to look down at the picture. "Oh, good eye, Cole." Smiling, she stared steadily at him. "You remembered these, and you'd only seen them for a minute last night."

"Yeah," he said, almost sighing in relief. She was going to help him out.

Then she walked away.

Robbie's stare remained as unwavering as Tina's had been.

Cole racked his brain, trying to recall what he had seen when he was with her that had been as colorful as the boy's scrawled picture.

Not her dark hair or her dark eyes or the plain blue shirt she had worn. Not any of the food they'd eaten at the campfire or even the fire itself. Definitely not the white afghan tossed on the arm of the couch in the attic. Not the covers of her books, spine-out on the shelves.

Then he had it.

He tilted his head and nodded, copying the movement Tina had made that morning when she claimed she was figuring things out. "Of course I know what this is. It's a butterfly."

Robbie grinned. "Yeah!" He held up his hand for a high five. "I knowed you would guess it. Daddies are smart."

Cole's heart skipped too many beats.

A new silence settled around them. This one went on forever. Or maybe it just seemed that way because he'd felt everything close in.

"'Daddies?'" he asked finally, his voice a croak.

"Yeah."

He waited.

Evidently feeling he had given a sufficient answer, Robbie reached for a crayon. Beside him, Scott had moved on to a drawing of a purple turtle—maybe—with yellow stripes.

Cole set his mug very gently on the table. "Did your mama...?" He cleared his throat and tried again. "Why did you say 'daddies?' Did your mama tell you to call me that?"

"Huh-uh." Robbie shook his head.

"How about your grandpa?"

"Nope. I just make it pretend."

"Oh." He paused, then asked, "Why did you do that?"

Robbie shrugged. "Rachel has a daddy and Scott has *two* daddies...sometimes." He paused and looked up at Cole. "I don't have a daddy. So I *have* to make it pretend."

Cole nodded. Amazing logic, especially coming from a four-year-old.

But then, Robbie was Tina's child, too.

THE AFTERNOON HAD almost slipped away by the time Tina returned from her ride and dismounted at the barn.

She thought again of the invitation she had extended to Cole earlier that morning. If he had accepted, the two of them could have been relaxing at a restaurant tonight. Instead, things had turned out much differently from what she had hoped. And she would have to face him in the dining room of the Hitching Post without Jane and Andi there to run interference.

When Pete came from the barn, she reluctantly turned the reins over to him. "I could take care of grooming Starlight."

He shook his head. "You'd better get over to the main house. With your cousins gone, Jed's been dragging his heels between here and there all afternoon, carving a rut in the ground. Looking for you, I expect."

Or for Cole.

But he had said he was spending most of the day in town.

"Jed misses Andi and Jane and the kids already," she said, knowing how he must feel. A few days ago, he had missed them when they hadn't even left yet. The way she would now miss Cole, whether he was here on the ranch or not. Whatever bond they might have forged between them last night was broken. "I think my *abuelo* might need a little extra attention."

"He's not the only one," Pete said. "Rachel's not herself today, either."

"She misses Trey?"

"I don't know." He frowned. "Usually, I can't get her to quiet down, but right now, she's not saying a word."

"I'll make sure she and Robbie have some playtime tomorrow."

"That would be great, thanks."

Turning away, she looked at her watch. It was early for dinner, but she would go home and freshen up in case Abuela and Maria needed help.

She hadn't made it halfway to the hotel before she saw Cole's pickup truck coast around the corner. It was early for him to be back, too.

He must have seen her, because the instant he climbed from the truck, he headed her way. "Got a minute?" he called.

She nodded and went over to the benches outside the corral to wait for him.

When he walked up to her, she said, "You're back early."

"Yeah."

"Then you're here for dinner?" It would be an intimate group at their table. At least Cole could focus his attention on Robbie again.

This morning at SugarPie's, she had deliberately left him at the table with the boys to give him more time to spend directly with their son. That's what he had wanted all along.

But he shook his head. "We grabbed something to eat

at the apartment. I'm glad I caught you out here. I wanted to talk. Alone."

She waited. His unemotional tone didn't necessarily mean this would be an awkward conversation. And what if it did? According to Ally, she was the queen of seriousness. She *enjoyed* discussing weighty topics...when they didn't involve her heart.

He shoved his Stetson back from his forehead and crossed his arms over his chest. "There's no point in wandering a trail to get to where I'm headed, so I'll just say it. I want to tell Robbie I'm his daddy."

Her heart skipped. She linked her unsteady fingers together in front of her. If ever she needed a time to rely on logic and forget emotion, this was it. "You mean," she said carefully, "you want to be Robbie's daddy."

"Yeah. It's time to tell him the truth."

"And that's it? You're deciding it's time, after all these years? Well, maybe if you hadn't walked away from me—"

"Don't." He sliced the air between them with his hand. "Don't try that line again, and don't blame it all on me. We've had this out before. You could have told me before I left, once you found out you were pregnant. And speaking of years, you've had the same number of them to reach me through Layne—if you'd really wanted me to know."

"And now *you're* making the decision, all on your own? Despite the fact I'm his mother and less than a month ago, he had never met you?" She tightened her fingers, hoping to hold on to her rising anger. And failing. "All along, you've said you were willing to wait. So, why is it time now? What changed?"

"He'll have questions," he shot back. "Lots of questions. And they're going to start soon. What will you tell him when that happens? Do you want him to think his daddy didn't care about him at all?"

At his final words, the blood drained from her face, leaving her dizzy. She had said something similar once, one night in a pickup truck near the high-school baseball field, when she told him how she felt about her parents abandoning her.

And now he'd taken those words, her confidences, her trust, and thrown them all in her face.

The verbal slap reminded her there was nothing between them any more. She needed to look out for her son. She jumped to her feet. "I'll answer Robbie's questions, the way I have since he was born. And just for the record, rushing to tell him you're his father makes it plain you *don't* care about him. Not enough. Why try to pretend you do?"

She moved aside, needing to get away from him, wanting to be alone.

He put his hand on her arm.

"'Pretend?'" he said hoarsely. "I'll tell you about pretend. Do you know Robbie's making up stories that I'm his daddy?"

Her breath caught. "He couldn't be. He doesn't know."

"He knows he doesn't have a daddy, like Scott and Rachel do. He told me that's why he pretends. Don't you think having a make-believe family could hurt him worse than knowing the truth?"

Chapter Seventeen

Cole begged off joining everyone in the dining room for supper. He couldn't have managed downing a cup of coffee, anyway, or sitting there and making small talk. Not when he knew what lay ahead.

He hadn't known how Tina would react when he insisted on talking to Robbie. He had never thought her feelings about the issue would affect him one way or the other. But to his surprise, he had cared about how she would feel.

He cared about Robbie, too, more than he ever would have thought possible. He wanted the boy to know the truth.

And he sure didn't want the next man in Tina's life to be his son's pretend daddy.

Out at the corral, he and Tina had managed to step back and take a breather. They had looked at things from another perspective. The most important perspective.

Robbie's.

He had pushed home the fact that an imaginary daddy could only hurt their son. Tina had looked stricken at that statement. But for Robbie's sake, she had agreed to let him talk to the boy.

While Jed and the others were still at the supper table, Cole went upstairs to her attic room. They had acknowledged this was the one place in the hotel where they could likely have their conversation without interruption.

He sat on the couch they had shared the night before and looked around the room. He thought about what could have happened in here if they hadn't stopped at those few little kisses. If he had taken her right here.

But he'd let the thought of having sex with her drive him once before, and look where it had gotten them.

His focus now had to be on what he would have to say in the very near future. He scrubbed his face with his hand as if the action could clear his head.

Dang. He hadn't been this nervous since he'd stood waiting in that Vegas wedding chapel.

Hearing footsteps on the stairs, he dropped his hand to his knee and sat frozen.

A moment later, Robbie padded into the room barefoot and wearing a pair of pajamas imprinted with pictures of robots and planets. "Hi," he said, his voice squeaking in surprise.

"Hey, Robbie."

Tina carried a tray with a carafe and a few mugs on it. She set it on the coffee table.

Robbie knelt at the table and dropped a coloring book and a box of crayons beside the tray. "Mama didn't tell me you was coming, too."

"She didn't, huh?" He shot a glance at Tina. They hadn't said much of anything once they had returned to the hotel. And they sure hadn't touched base on how the heck he would handle this.

"Would you like some hot chocolate?" she asked him, holding up the carafe.

"*With* marshmallers," Robbie added. "Just like the s'mores, only small."

"That sounds good." He started to gesture toward the

coloring book, then stopped, recalling the conversation at SugarPie's that morning. Then, Tina had given him a hint about Robbie's drawing. He wouldn't bet on her doing that now.

He took the mug she handed him and sat back on the couch. "You liked the s'mores last night, huh? And the muffins this morning?"

"Yeah. Chocolate is the best." Robbie dumped the crayons from the box onto the table.

"You remember after you had the muffins and we were talking about your picture? Do you remember what you said?"

He nodded. "I knowed you would guess. I made a butterfly like Mama's—there." He pointed to Tina's collection on the corner shelf, then began scribbling on a page in his coloring book.

"Do you remember what else you said?"

His hand stilled. "Maybe." He looked warily from Cole to Tina.

"You do remember?" Tina prompted.

"I said...I said..." He bit his lip.

Cole reached out and ruffled his hair. "Hey, that's okay. I remember. You said daddies are smart."

"I know." He looked at Tina. "Mamas are smart, too!"

Her laugh seemed to hitch in the middle. "Of course they are. Smart enough to know when a boy wants hot chocolate."

Cole sipped from his mug. She *was* smart. Shrewd. And so danged proud.

He couldn't help but wonder how she was going to take the news he had to tell Jed. Presenting the offer to the old man would have to wait till the morning. He'd need the rest of tonight to recover from the conversation he was about to have right now.

This time, when he lifted his mug, his hand wasn't quite as steady.

Tina poured some chocolate into a small mug with a lid. Robbie took it and held it out toward Cole. "Like the pop."

To celebrate winning at horseshoes, he and Robbie had shared a drink and tapped their bottles together—Robbie's pop and his beer. Now Cole touched his mug against the smaller one.

He hesitated, not sure how to lead into this. But the kid was four years old. Long explanations weren't required. "Since you said daddies are smart, I wanted to tell you something."

"About the surprise?"

Cole looked at Tina.

"I told Robbie he might have a surprise waiting up here."

He took a deep breath and let it out again. "Yeah, it is about the surprise. I wanted to tell you, you have a daddy, too."

"Like Rachel and Scott?"

"Yeah."

"That's good. Now I won't make it pretend, right?"

"Right. And I won't, either. Because I'm your daddy."

Robbie grinned. "That's good," he said again and reached up to give him a high five. Then he picked up his mug. "Mama, when I drink up all my chocolate, can I have the surprise?"

ONCE SHE HAD tucked Robbie into bed, Tina made her way up the stairs to her attic sanctuary for the second time that evening. And again, as arranged, Cole would be there waiting for her.

Robbie had taken the news about Cole so calmly, they had agreed to let things stand for now.

They had come to that decision simply enough. She had raised her eyebrows in question, and he had shrugged, then given a nonchalant nod—as if they had long ago developed a mode of nonverbal parenting.

No, the conversation hadn't fazed Robbie much.

She couldn't say the same for herself. Or for Cole.

He sat in the same position on the couch as when she had left to take Robbie downstairs.

"Did he buy the story about your cookies being the surprise?"

"Yes." Thank goodness she had left the package up here a couple of nights ago.

She poured herself some hot chocolate and went to sit on a chair out of tempting reach of him but close enough to see his expression. "Cole..." She gripped the mug in her lap. "Before you talked with Robbie, when you were drinking your chocolate, your hand was shaking."

Her sigh verged on a sob, just as her laugh had done when Robbie had so carefully assured her mamas were smart, too.

"I was wrong earlier, and I'm sorry. You certainly cared about how Robbie was going to react when you told him you were his daddy."

He shrugged. "It's not a conversation I've had before."

"The point is, you wanted the conversation. You wanted your relationship with Robbie out in the open." Her voice cracked. She pushed on. "That has to mean something, no matter what you tell me about not wanting a family."

He looked down at his mug and said nothing.

She rose and walked across the room, standing with her back to him. Then she squared her shoulders. He was going to walk away from her again. But this time, she wouldn't let him leave on his terms. "I was also wrong for saying I could handle all his questions. Because I don't know all the answers."

She turned to face him again and said quietly, "There's one answer I'd like to know now. Not for Robbie. For me. How can you care so much about our son and still say you don't want a family?"

Cole wanted to laugh at the irony in the situation.

Tina, normally so calm and quiet, became a spitfire whenever Robbie was at risk. And he, who always liked to keep on the move, suddenly couldn't move at all.

The accusation in her eyes might have pinned him against his seat.

Finally, he said, "I'm not cut out to raise a child."

"Your actions lately seem to contradict that."

"That's in the short term. Not the same as living with kids day-to-day."

"The more you're around them, the better you get at being a parent."

"The longer the time," he countered, "the shorter the fuse."

"What?" She frowned in confusion. "I don't think that's the issue here."

"You didn't have a dad like mine."

Her face paled.

Damn.

At the corral a few hours ago, and again just now, he'd said exactly the things guaranteed to hurt her. Sure, their circumstances growing up had been different. She hadn't had a dad at all. But the point was, he hadn't taken her feelings into account. He'd been a jackass, twice over. He had to make up for that.

And, bottom line, as the mother of his child, she deserved to hear his whole history.

No matter how reluctant he was to share it.

"My dad was never meant to have kids," he said flatly. "He had no interest, no patience and zero attention span at home except for watching TV. My mother wasn't a whole lot better. Layne and I pretty much raised ourselves."

"That doesn't mean you'd behave the same way," she protested.

"*That* was heaven in a handbasket, compared to the rest." He tapped the mug on his knee. "When we bothered my dad too much—like asking him for more milk—he'd get loud. Nasty. I'd always give him backtalk. Until I learned if I didn't shut up, he would turn on Layne. She couldn't argue as well as I could. Hell, how could she? When he started in on her, she could barely talk at all. I was four years old. She was only two."

Tina's eyes glittered.

He blinked and looked down at his mug.

"After that, I let him say whatever he wanted to me, to keep him away from her. I stuck it out at home, too, long after I'd have gone out on my own. Fourteen years of hearing I was a rotten brother and son…well, that's something I could leave behind. But taking the chance of being like the dad he was…"

He stood and placed his mug of now-cold chocolate on the tray she'd left on the coffee table.

"I'd have been better off never having a dad."

Chapter Eighteen

Until now, Cole's bed at the Hitching Post had suited him fine. But all his admissions in last night's conversation with Tina had made it impossible for him to sleep.

Good thing Jed was an early riser.

Downstairs, he found the man with his feet propped up on the desk in his den and a newspaper in his hands.

When he saw him in the doorway, Jed tossed the newspaper aside. "Well, what are you doing up before Paz even has breakfast on the griddle?"

He took a seat in the cracked leather chair in front of the desk and set his Stetson on his knee. "I'm here to offer you a proposition."

Jed gave him a huge grin. "Are you, now? I think you might be presenting it to the wrong person."

"No, I'm not." The man meant Tina.

Tina, the woman who wanted everything from him. She always had, ever since their school days. Love, marriage, a family. After last night, maybe she understood why some of that was impossible.

As she was the person handling the financial end of the renovations, he could have laid out the offer to her. But considering the situation between them, it was probably better that Jed pass along the news.

The old man sat back and put his hands behind his head. "Fire away."

He presented the uncomplicated details. "I'm not going into this to rake in cash, and my partners are in full agreement with the low interest rate. I'll be pleased to be helping you out, if you accept the offer."

"I'll give it some thought," Jed said, nodding.

"Then I'll follow up with you in a few days." He ran his thumb over the crown of his Stetson. "I've got another reason for stopping in. I wanted to let you know I'm planning on leaving—but this time I'm giving notice."

"Leaving?" Jed dropped his feet to the floor and sat forward. "What about Tina?"

"What about her?"

"Don't play the fool with me, boy. I know there's something happening between the two of you. And so you're up and running off again because of it?"

"I'm not running or even leaving town. Layne still needs me here. I just won't be working on the ranch. As for Tina..." He tried for a smile but failed. "Whatever was happening between the two of us is history."

"And what's going to happen from here on is called the future. One that affects me and Paz and your son."

Feeling the need to pace, he rose from the chair. "Then maybe you can understand what it was like not to learn about my son until he was four years old."

"I understand more than you know. You've heard about Tina's parents?"

"I heard they gave her away to Paz and left town. She told me that...a long time ago."

"Yeah," Jed said. "Well, it took Paz a while to get around to giving me the news years ago, too. She didn't tell me Tina was my granddaughter until the girl was older than

Robbie is now. Tina didn't know for a while after that, either."

That stopped him in his tracks. "Are you saying that's a reason to forgive her for not telling me?"

"I'm saying all folks run into situations they have to handle the best they can at the time. The way you tried to provide for your sister."

Tina had said the same thing about his choice to let Layne get married so young.

"And," Jed went on, "I'm saying folks who don't do their best with what life brings them can find themselves having some very big regrets." Jed rose from his chair. "I think I'll go check and see if Paz has my breakfast ready. Since I'll be taking a few days to give your offer some thought, why don't you do the same about giving notice?"

TINA HAD TOLD Pete she would give Rachel some playtime with Robbie. The kids had had such a good afternoon, she decided to bring them along with her when she met with Ally. She didn't mind having their company on the ride into town. Their chatter in the car helped to keep her from thinking of Cole.

When they reached Canyon Road Tina made a detour and parked outside SugarPie's.

Robbie looked through the car window. "Not muffins, Mama. Ice cream!"

"I know, sweetie. We're just going to stop and have something to drink before we meet Aunt Ally."

Ally had had a disappointing weekend with her wrangler. Tina hadn't heard the details yet but knew things couldn't be good when Ally insisted they skip their walk and go straight to the Big Dipper.

Before they met, Tina hoped for a chat with Cole's sister. Inside SugarPie's, she chose a small table for two as far from the rest of the diners as possible and settled Rachel and Robbie there with place mats and crayons. Then she took a seat at the next table.

From across the room, Layne gave her a wave, acknowledging she'd seen her.

Tina didn't know what reason Cole had given her about his stay at the Hitching Post. But after brunch here the other day, she was certain he had now told his sister about Robbie.

When Layne had delivered their order for one cup of tea and two apple juices, Tina said, "Could you sit for a minute?"

"Sure."

"I'm glad Cole has been able to bring Scott out to the Hitching Post."

"I am, too. Scott talks constantly about his new friends, especially Robbie."

"And Robbie has been having a great time playing with him. That's why I wanted to chat. My cousins went home again, and I don't come in to town all that often. I...don't like to ask Cole to play chauffeur all the time, but I'd like to make sure the boys still have the chance to get together. I thought maybe we could set up a few play dates and I'd schedule them on my hotel calendar."

"That would be great. I'd like to have Robbie come over and visit us, too. I need to get to know him better. And you." She smoothed the sheets of her order pad. "We didn't see very much of each other in school."

"That's not surprising. There were two years between us." The comment reminded her of the conversation she'd had with Andi, though in her own case, she hadn't avoided Layne deliberately. "And once I graduated, I was busy between college and working at the hotel."

"And I was busy making a mess of a couple of marriages." Layne grimaced. "I don't know if Cole mentioned this," she said in a lower voice, "but he told me about Robbie. I'm glad he did. And I hope you don't mind. Cole's a wonderful brother, Tina. He'll be a wonderful daddy." She fiddled with the order pad. "He wouldn't like me saying this, but you should know. He and I come with a lot of baggage. You're shy, I know—or at least, you always were. When it comes to marriage and family, he's gun-shy, and that's a whole different story."

"That doesn't matter as far as Scott and Robbie are concerned." She meant the words, yet her smile felt brittle. "There's no reason we can't set up those play dates."

"And no reason we can't be friends."

After Layne had gone to take care of her customers, Tina sat sipping her tea and thinking of Cole.

She wished he could believe in himself as much as Layne believed in him.

The story he had told her about their home life had broken her heart. After listening to that story, after seeing the look on his face and hearing the finality in his tone, she knew there was no point in holding on to her dreams. She would never have her big family with Cole.

And she feared he could never truly love the son they already shared.

COLE'S WALK DOWN Canyon Road took longer than it would have normally. Scott walked along beside him and stopped every few feet to investigate a store window, sort of like a puppy sniffing every clump of grass.

At this rate, they wouldn't get where they were going and back to the apartment before Layne got home from SugarPie's.

Knowing he needed some distance from Tina, he had decided to have supper with Scott. Layne was working the evening shift tonight, and he had assured her he could manage to heat up a can of spaghetti.

The unappetizing meal had turned him off, but Scott enjoyed chasing mini-meatballs around on his plate. Sure he knew what else his nephew would like, he'd stowed the dishes in the dishwasher and said, "Ice cream?"

And here they were.

He pulled open the heavy glass door and let Scott scurry in ahead of him.

At a corner table, he saw Robbie and Rachel. And Tina.

Robbie spotted them instantly. His huge grin made Cole's heart thump in a good way.

Tina's unsmiling gaze just made his heart thump.

There was no way for him to avoid her, since Scott had already climbed up into an empty chair at their table.

"Hey," he said. "Is this a party?"

"Just dessert. Ally's supposed to meet us here at any minute."

"We're out for some ice cream." *Well, yeah*.

"Then you've come to the right place."

She kept a straight face, but he caught the gleam in her eye. He hadn't had a conversation this stilted with a female since first grade.

Come to think of it, that might have been with Tina, too.

The door opened again, stirring the refrigerated air in the room. He looked in that direction and saw her friend Ally entering the shop. He also saw the man who held the door for her, waiting to make his exit.

"Excuse me," he said to Tina and the kids.

He strode across the room, nodded hello to Ally, then grabbed the door just before it shut.

Outside, he picked up his pace a notch to grab the shoulder of the man walking in front of him. When he swung him around, the guy almost dropped the white paper sack he was carrying.

"Out for some ice cream, Terry?" he asked. This time, his words weren't stilted. The one he muttered under his breath wouldn't have been fit for the ice cream shop. "It would have been nice of you to think of Scott, considering you've stood him up a few times."

"I didn't know if he was home or not. Or if Layne was working."

"You ever hear of something called the telephone?"

"Very funny. Back off, Cole." Terry narrowed his watery blue eyes and raised his poor excuse for a jaw.

Cole wondered what Layne had ever seen in him. He took a step forward, herding Terry toward the curb. "You want my cell number? No problem. Then you won't have to worry about Layne's schedule, and we can make sure you and Scott have some time together. You want time with Scott, don't you?"

Terry said nothing, just sent his gaze toward the ice cream shop.

Cole sidestepped into his line of vision again. "What kind of man makes promises to a kid and then won't deliver? What kind of creep invites a three-year-old for ice cream and then doesn't show?"

"Hey. I was trying to do Layne a favor and something came up—"

"Twice?"

"That's not even my kid—"

"*That* is Layne's son. All right, he's not yours. What does that matter? You've raised him, you piece—"

"Cole."

"—of crap. What's your attitude gonna be once the baby comes along?" He moved closer, until Terry backed off onto the street. "You're divorced—"

"Cole."

"—so you can hand over the responsibility? If I didn't know the baby was yours, I'd tell Layne to—"

"Cole!"

He felt a tug on the back of his shirt and spun around. Tina stood on the sidewalk just a foot from him. Her golden-tan skin had faded to a shade almost as pale as his nephew's.

"The kids are watching," she said in a low voice.

He shot a glance toward the shop. Inside, all three kids and Ally sat looking through the front window. Luckily, the couple of other customers and the girl scooping ice cream seemed too busy at the counter to notice. He forced a smile and gave the kids a wave.

They waved back.

He shot another glance over his shoulder and saw Terry climbing into a pickup truck. He turned back to Tina, resettled his hat and made himself meet her gaze. "Guess I just gave you the perfect example of how much I take after my dad."

"Your dad wouldn't have picked on someone his own size. And you *were* defending Scott. But as for the way you made your point—"

"Yeah, well, I suppose I could've kept it more civil. I got a little carried away talking to that creep."

"So I heard."

"How much? Did you hear the part about him promising to take Scott for ice cream and then reneging?"

She nodded. "That's about where I came in. Or out, I should say. And that's what I meant about making your point. You had good intentions, but this wasn't the time or place—"

"No? Wouldn't you have done the same if he'd let down our son?"

He heard her breath catch. To his dismay, her eyes began to tear.

"'Our son?'" She blinked hard and shook her head. "I know this isn't the time or the place, either, Cole...but I have to tell you this before I say what else I need to say. I love you. I have always loved you. And I won't believe you don't already know that." She crossed her arms.

He felt his chest tighten.

"Robbie's only 'our son' to you when it's convenient," she said sadly. "I don't mind at all that you're spending time with Scott, so please don't think that's what this is about. But I want to know—I *need* to know—what the future's going to be like for Robbie...with you.

"Yesterday you told him you were his daddy, and today you weren't even around to say hello. Is that what he has to look forward to? Like Scott with Terry?" Her voice broke.

She glanced away from him and took a deep breath.

He swallowed hard and tried to keep his gaze from the shop window. By the time she looked back at him, he had managed to regain some composure.

"I'm sorry," she said softly, "*so* sorry—for what you went through growing up. It sounds like you're right. It would have been better for you and Layne not to have a father at all.

"And maybe Robbie would be better off without you, too."

The pain in her eyes made him want to reach for her, but he couldn't seem to move.

"Layne believes in you," she said. "I believe in you. But I don't think you'll ever be a real daddy to Robbie unless *you* truly believe in you."

Chapter Nineteen

After breakfast, Tina went to her office to gather the files she needed.

It had been three days since her trip to town, and she hadn't seen Cole at all. That night, after his run-in with Terry and then his conversation with her, he had purchased a container of ice cream to go at the Big Dipper, then he and Scott had left the shop.

Robbie and Rachel had gone to a separate table close by, leaving Tina and Ally in the quiet corner.

When Ally asked, Tina repeated most of what had happened between Cole and Terry. She didn't say much at all about her near-monologue with Cole afterward. Ally would have seen it, but she didn't press for details. Out of sympathy, Tina knew—although Ally did spend a while sharing details of her own.

As her best friend had put it, "We're a great pair, Tina. Your cute cowboy is marriage-shy, and my cute wrangler is already married."

She had proceeded to drown her sorrows in her triple-dip fudge sundae.

Tina's ice cream cone hadn't provided any comfort at all. She doubted anything could.

She grabbed the file folders from her desk. Jed, who had watched her so closely for days now, had noticed something wrong. Though she wasn't looking forward to her upcoming meeting with him, she didn't have a choice.

When she tracked him down in his den, she found him sitting with a file folder of his own on the desk. "Wanted to talk to you about something," he said gruffly.

"Okay."

"The other day, Cole made me an offer regarding the hotel."

For a moment, her *abuelo*'s flat-out straight delivery method left her breathless. When she could finally speak, her words came out in a croak. "An offer?" *To buy the hotel?*

Her hopes soared.

Did his offer to Jed prove he cared about her? Had he made this effort to show her what he couldn't seem to tell her?

But serious, level-headed Tina had to squash those emotion-filled questions. "What kind of offer?"

"An investment to help with the renovations."

"I see."

She listened, half her mind taking his words in as he explained Cole's plan to pool resources with some friends. The other half of her mind could barely cope with the knowledge she had left herself vulnerable to Cole yet again.

"I told him I'd give him an answer in a few days."

She nodded.

"And I'm turning down their offer. They can keep their money."

She frowned. "I hope you're not making that decision because of something to do with me."

Jed waved her concern away. "If that boy doesn't have the brains he was born with, how could I trust him or his friends?"

"Then we've got a problem, Abuelo. We're not going to be able to afford a third of the renovations you want done—unless you're willing to take a look at this proposal." She slid the paperwork from the file folder and placed it on the desk in front of him.

He barely glanced at the file. "Run it by me."

"I've worked up a budget, but it's based on a short-term loan. I know you won't be happy to hear it's got interest attached. But I've got a great rate we should be able to handle easily. And the loan amount is enough to see the hotel through to completion."

"If you say it's what we need, that's good enough for me."

She sighed. She *needed* more than that. Much more. And it had nothing to do with the hotel.

Still, she was glad for his acceptance, as it would make everything go more smoothly for the renovations.

One of them, at least, would have a dream come true.

COLE BROKE DOWN the last of Layne's packing boxes and looked at her across the living room. She stood at an ironing board, pressing curtains.

"Now that I'm finally getting these up," she said, "the place might start feeling like a home."

She and Tina had the same nesting instincts. "It already feels like a home to me."

"Thanks." She smiled. "If I had known you were planning to spend your Saturday with us, I wouldn't have set up a play date for Scott today. I can call Tina and cancel."

"No, don't do that. I'm glad the boys get to see each other. They get along well."

"It's nice for Scott to have so many new cousins, too."

She transferred the curtain to a rod and handed it to

him. As he came down the ladder, she gestured around the room. "What do you think? Haven't we done a great job?"

"You've done most of the work. I was just the helper."

"Oh, no, you weren't. You were here every step of the way. You've always been here for me. I don't want to push, but I hope you know, I'm here for you, too. And in case you're wondering, when I've seen Tina at the shop this week, she hasn't said a word about you."

"That supposed to make me feel good?"

"You know what I mean."

He paced toward the end of the living room to look through the kitchen doorway. Scott sat at the table, busy for the moment with his coloring book.

The chance to talk to Layne alone was too good to pass up. He paced back toward her.

Nothing could ease his need to move. He just wished he had more space in the small living room. Like that one afternoon by the corral when he'd had the boys pretending to be lions, he wished he could run off to the jungle.

The art of pretending seemed to run in his family.

She frowned. "Everything all right? You seem tense."

"I am tense." He tried to ease his tight jaw. "When I first found out about Robbie, I told Tina I wanted him to have the chance to get to know me before I told him I was his daddy. That's as far as we got." Loath to bring up a touchy subject for Layne, he hesitated, then finally admitted, "We never talked about support. But naturally I'm going to be responsible for my kid."

"Of course you would feel that way. Unlike a lot of other men."

He winced every time he thought of how he'd confronted her ex at the ice cream shop. But once she heard the story, Layne told him she was writing Terry off. She had to think of Scott. And to consider her pride.

Tina had her pride, too, and lots of it. Like Jed, she would probably want to settle things with a handshake. He wouldn't accept that.

But to tell the truth, he didn't like the thought of discussing these subjects with her at all. He didn't like the idea of anything that would raise more barriers between them.

No matter how much she'd stressed to him that her concerns were for their son, he could see that forever look in her eyes. Or maybe he just wanted to know she still believed in forever.

Then he thought about what she wanted *him* to believe...

And made himself stop right there.

"I've told her the truth all along," he said. "I'm not marriage *or* daddy material."

"Please don't sell yourself short." Layne's voice broke. "You always do, and I know why. But it's not true. Don't you see that taking care of me, watching out for me the way you did, trained you be a wonderful husband and daddy?"

She brushed at her eyes. Then she gave him a wry smile. "Listen, I may have picked a couple of bad apples in the past, but at least that's taught me how to look for the good ones in the barrel. And I've never had trouble seeing you're a great man."

"I don't know about that." He gestured at the room around them. "Maybe if I'd done a better job saying no to you the first time, you'd wouldn't be in this place now."

"That's on me, not you. You can't let my bad choices worry you. And if you hadn't let me make those choices, I wouldn't have Scott."

"There is that," he agreed. "You're a good mom." *Like Tina.* He had to be truthful about that.

"And I'm going to be a good wife to somebody again." She crossed the room and rested her hand on his arm.

"Mom and Dad are long gone. But if we refuse to hold out hope for happy-ever-afters, we'll be letting them ruin our lives. And our kids' lives. And," she said very softly, "you'll be ruining Tina's life, too. We can't let any of that happen, Cole. We're *all* worth more than that."

TINA AND ROBBIE arrived ahead of schedule at the miniature golf course on the outskirts of Cowboy Creek. She had taken a seat in the shade near the registration desk.

During the past fifteen minutes, Robbie had run to the grassy strip beside the parking lot more times than she could count.

"Here you go, Robbie. Why don't you buy our scorecards?"

"For Scott and his mama, too?"

"Yes." She handed him the exact change and watched as he walked to the registration desk. As usual this early, the golf course was quiet. The transaction didn't take long, and he started toward the parking lot again.

"Running back and forth isn't going to bring Scott and his mom here any faster," she called.

Running every conversation she'd had with Cole through her head over and over wouldn't bring him back, either. And still, she couldn't stop herself. She couldn't keep from wondering where he had been all week, either. Since Monday, he hadn't come for dinner in the dining room at all. More than likely, he ate at Layne's or Sugar-Pie's or even the Lucky Strike.

When she had tried to find out from Jed, he had muttered something about absence making her heart grow fonder. She didn't tell Abuelo her heart had already broken.

"You're wrong, Mama!" Robbie shouted. He ran up to her, his eyes wide in astonishment. "I brought Scott *and* I brought my daddy."

"Oh, honey, I don't think so."

"Yes, Mama. Look right there."

Despite warning herself that Robbie had to be mistaken, she couldn't stop the way her miraculously restored heart raced. She turned to look and saw Cole and Scott approaching.

Scott ran ahead of Cole, and both boys went to get their golf clubs.

Cole stopped a few feet away and shoved his hands in his back pockets.

"I...didn't expect you," she said. "Are you planning to stay or just dropping Scott off?"

"Staying. If you're not afraid of being compromised."

She hesitated, then finally said, "There are a few things I'm afraid of, but being compromised by you isn't one of them."

"Sounds good." He looked at the desk. "Clubs over there?"

"Clubs there. Scorecards here." She held up the extras.

He plucked them from her hand.

"Is Layne okay?"

"Yeah. I told her I'd fill in for her today."

"Oh. I didn't know when I'd get the chance to talk to you again. I'm glad you're here." She clutched the second pair of scorecards. "Before we join the boys, I just wanted to say I've been doing a lot of thinking. I owe you an apology for not telling you about Robbie. You were right. I could have reached you through Layne. And I should have."

She took a deep breath, then continued. "I meant what I'd said to you. It breaks my heart to think I don't know how much you'll ever be capable of loving Robbie. But you *are* his daddy. And I won't stand in your way. No matter how big or small a role you want to play, you deserve to be a part of his life."

"I do want a part in his life. A big one."

His admission thrilled her. "I'm glad for that, too. Sincerely."

The boys ran up to them. Over their heads, Cole smiled at her and she smiled back.

She'd spent her entire life, or so it seemed, loving Cole and letting him see everything she was thinking. Everything that was in her heart. But she never could read him the same way. And she wouldn't jump to conclusions about what he wanted now.

Robbie took her hand. "C'mon, Mama. C'mon, Daddy. You've gotta get your sticks."

There wasn't time for any personal conversation as they worked their way around the course. Cole helped Robbie with his putts and Robbie in his turn helped Scott. She followed them, happy to be with them all.

When the first game was finished and the boys wanted another, Tina agreed but said, "I'll sit this one out." She took a seat on the bench in the center of the course and watched.

After a while, Cole told the boys to go on ahead of him. He came over to sit beside her.

"You play as well as the boys do," she said.

"Well, I'm not up to par today."

She groaned. "Bad pun."

"I am a player, though. Or at least, I was. That's something you were right about in school. Calling me a playboy." He tapped the toe of his boot with his club. "All I wanted was to play. To have fun. To avoid getting serious. All I lived for was the day I could get out of Cowboy Creek. Now you know about my family, maybe you can understand."

"I do."

He shook his head. "And then there was you. The most serious girl I'd ever met.

"Even in grade school, I used to see you looking at me with those big brown eyes, all solemn. And as they say, I could read you like a book. I wasn't kidding about seeing you were a forever kinda girl. And after seriousness, if there was one thing I didn't do, it was forever.

"Then we got thrown together in high school, and things led to those nights we spent talking in the truck. The night we slept together, I knew I was in big trouble. Because you'd gotten me started thinking about the future."

He tapped his boot again, looked over at the boys, shifted his Stetson and, finally, gave a heavy sigh.

"Tina, the next day, when you asked me to the Sadie Hawkins dance, I panicked. Because I knew what you expected, and it was so much more than a dance and so much more than I could ever give you.

"My dad drummed that into me, telling me over and over again I wasn't worth much."

"Just because he said it doesn't mean it has to define you. I used to think, because my parents had abandoned me, I wasn't worth loving. I wasn't worth anything. I know that's not true. And I always knew Abuela and Jed loved me. But I convinced myself no one else would. I had to learn to believe in myself."

He shrugged. "Well, I guess I never got to that stage, till now. But while I was working on getting there, hearing you say the other day that you believe in me was one of the best things that ever happened to me." He reached for her hand and squeezed her fingers. "Telling me I deserve to be part of Robbie's life is, too."

She smiled.

A few yards away, the boys wrapped up their game.

They came pounding across the turf, shrieking with pleasure, and skidded to a stop in front of the bench.

"I'm the big winner!" Robbie shouted.

"And Scott's the little winner, right?" Cole asked.

"Right! Can we play again?"

Cole looked at her.

She nodded.

Robbie grinned, and the boys ran back to start their game.

"He's got your smile," Cole said, touching her chin.

"He's got your eyes."

"You know, all these years, I've been restless, keeping on the move—on the run, Jed says. But when I came back here, I felt settled. And that's because of you." He smiled. "If there's one thing I know about you, shy, quiet Tina, it's that you've got a lot of pride. And when the situation wasn't the best, I saw you push that pride away to tell me you loved me."

He took a deep breath and let it out again. "I can't do any less than push away the things I've always feared to tell you some things, too. I don't want to feel restless. I don't want to be on the run. I just want to be home again. With you."

"That's all I've ever wanted."

He ran his finger down her cheek. "Even in high school, when I couldn't trust myself to get close to you, I had a crush on you."

She gasped. "You did?"

"I did. Now I love you." He wrapped his arm around her shoulders. "You're a forever kinda girl, Tina, and I want forever with you."

She rested her head on his shoulder. "Forever and a family?" she asked.

"Forever...and a *big* family," he agreed.

Epilogue

One month later

On his way to the kitchen, Jed detoured to make a stop at the doorway of the sitting room.

Cole and Tina sat snuggled close together on the couch. Yet neither of them looked a bit happy.

He frowned. "What's the matter?"

Tina bit her lip.

"Cole," he snapped. "What's going on?"

"Tina just told me she talked with Jane and Andi today. Once the wedding chapel's refurbished, they want Tina to be the first bride to be married there."

"Yeah, they told me that." He smiled. "I can't think of anything I'd like more."

"Yeah, well…" Cole ran his hand through his hair.

Frowning again, Jed slapped his hand on the door frame. "All right, you two. Out with it. Flat-out straight."

"Abuelo," Tina said, "I know you like the idea. I love it, too. And…" Her eyes filled with tears, but she was smiling.

Jed had to blink a time or two himself.

"And," she started again, "I love Andi and Jane for thinking of it. But the hotel rooms and the ballroom are my priorities. It will be months before we're ready to reopen the chapel." She rested her head against Cole's shoulder. "We don't want to wait that long."

"We've waited too long already," Cole said.

"I can sure attest to that. Well, it's your wedding. Whenever and wherever you want to tie the knot, I'll be there, ready to walk Tina down the aisle."

He left the two lovebirds alone and continued to the kitchen, where Paz was fixing supper.

Once he had poured himself a cup of coffee, he took his usual seat at the table. "I'll tell you, Paz, I'm about ready to dance a jig."

"Your plans have worked out just fine."

"That they have."

He was now the proprietor of a soon-to-be thriving hotel.

The lovebirds would stay under his roof—literally, since Tina was converting the attic into an apartment.

And with one of his granddaughters getting hitched, he only had two to go.

* * * * *

COMING NEXT MONTH FROM
HARLEQUIN
American Romance

Available May 5, 2015

#1545 THE COWBOY'S HOMECOMING
Crooked Valley Ranch • by Donna Alward

Rylan Duggan finds himself off the rodeo circuit and back at Crooked Valley Ranch—too close for comfort to Kailey Brandt. She's not about to forgive him for past wrongs, but their chemistry makes him impossible to ignore!

#1546 HER COWBOY GROOM
Blue Falls, Texas • by Trish Milburn

Linnea Holland doesn't trust men anymore. But cowboy Owen Brody shows he has a kind heart beneath his bad-boy exterior and makes her think she *can* trust him—and maybe even fall in love.

#1547 THE RANCHER'S LULLABY
Glades County Cowboys • by Leigh Duncan

Ranch manager and single father Garrett Judd still blames himself for his wife's death. But bluegrass singer Lisa Rose makes embracing life too hard to resist...at least for one stormy night.

#1548 BACK TO TEXAS
Welcome to Ramblewood • by Amanda Renee

Waitress Bridgett Jameson is done being the subject of small-town gossip. Falling for handsome, mysterious ranch hand Adam Steele seems like the perfect escape from Ramblewood...until she learns his secret!

YOU CAN FIND MORE INFORMATION ON UPCOMING HARLEQUIN® TITLES, FREE EXCERPTS AND MORE AT WWW.HARLEQUIN.COM.

REQUEST YOUR FREE BOOKS!
2 FREE NOVELS PLUS 2 FREE GIFTS!

HARLEQUIN

American Romance

LOVE, HOME & HAPPINESS

YES! Please send me 2 FREE Harlequin® American Romance® novels and my 2 FREE gifts (gifts are worth about $10). After receiving them, if I don't wish to receive any more books, I can return the shipping statement marked "cancel." If I don't cancel, I will receive 4 brand-new novels every month and be billed just $4.74 per book in the U.S. or $5.24 per book in Canada. That's a savings of at least 14% off the cover price! It's quite a bargain! Shipping and handling is just 50¢ per book in the U.S. and 75¢ per book in Canada.* I understand that accepting the 2 free books and gifts places me under no obligation to buy anything. I can always return a shipment and cancel at any time. Even if I never buy another book, the two free books and gifts are mine to keep forever.

154/354 HDN F4YN

Name	(PLEASE PRINT)	
Address		Apt. #
City	State/Prov.	Zip/Postal Code

Signature (if under 18, a parent or guardian must sign)

Mail to the Harlequin® Reader Service:
IN U.S.A.: P.O. Box 1867, Buffalo, NY 14240-1867
IN CANADA: P.O. Box 609, Fort Erie, Ontario L2A 5X3

Want to try two free books from another line?
Call 1-800-873-8635 or visit www.ReaderService.com.

* Terms and prices subject to change without notice. Prices do not include applicable taxes. Sales tax applicable in N.Y. Canadian residents will be charged applicable taxes. Offer not valid in Quebec. This offer is limited to one order per household. Not valid for current subscribers to Harlequin American Romance books. All orders subject to credit approval. Credit or debit balances in a customer's account(s) may be offset by any other outstanding balance owed by or to the customer. Please allow 4 to 6 weeks for delivery. Offer available while quantities last.

Your Privacy—The Harlequin® Reader Service is committed to protecting your privacy. Our Privacy Policy is available online at www.ReaderService.com or upon request from the Harlequin Reader Service.

We make a portion of our mailing list available to reputable third parties that offer products we believe may interest you. If you prefer that we not exchange your name with third parties, or if you wish to clarify or modify your communication preferences, please visit us at www.ReaderService.com/consumerschoice or write to us at Harlequin Reader Service Preference Service, P.O. Box 9062, Buffalo, NY 14269. Include your complete name and address.

HAR13R

SPECIAL EXCERPT FROM

HARLEQUIN

American Romance

Read on for a sneak preview of
HER COWBOY GROOM, the next book in
Trish Milburn's
*wonderful **BLUE FALL, TEXAS** series.*

Despite still feeling shaky, Linnea descended the steps and started walking. The day was quite warm, but she didn't care. Though she spent most of her time indoors working, there was something therapeutic about getting out in the sunshine under a wide blue sky. It almost made her believe things weren't so bad.

But they were.

She walked the length of the driveway and back. When she approached the house, Roscoe and Cletus, the Brodys' two lovable basset hounds, came ambling around the corner of the porch.

"Hey, guys," she said as she sank onto the front steps and proceeded to scratch them both under their chins. "You're just as handsome as ever."

"Why, thank you."

She jumped at the sound of Owen's voice. The dogs jumped, too, probably because she had. She glanced up to where Owen stood at the corner of the porch. "You made me scare the dogs."

"Sorry. But I was taught to thank someone when they pay me a compliment."

She shook her head. "Nice to see your ego is still intact."

"Ouch."

She laughed a little at his mock affront, something she wouldn't have thought possible that morning. She ought to thank him for that moment of reprieve, but she didn't want to focus on why she'd thought she might never laugh or even smile again.

He tapped the brim of his cowboy hat and headed toward the barn.

As he walked away, she noticed how nice he looked in those worn jeans. No wonder he didn't have trouble finding women.

Oh, hell! She was looking at Owen's butt. Owen, as in Chloe's little brother Owen. The kid who'd once waited on her and Chloe outside Chloe's room and doused them with a Super Soaker, the guy who had earned the nickname Horndog Brody.

She jerked her gaze away, suddenly wondering if she was mentally deficient. First she'd nearly married a guy who was already married. And now, little more than a day after she found out she'd nearly become an unwitting bigamist, she was ogling her best friend's brother's rear end.

Don't miss
HER COWBOY GROOM
by Trish Milburn,
available May 2015 wherever
Harlequin® American Romance®
books and ebooks are sold.

www.Harlequin.com

Copyright © 2015 by Trish Milburn

HARLEQUIN®
A *Romance* FOR EVERY MOOD™

Love the Harlequin book you just read?

Your opinion matters.

Review this book on your favorite book site, review site, blog or your own social media properties and share your opinion with other readers!

Be sure to connect with us at:
Harlequin.com/Newsletters
Facebook.com/HarlequinBooks
Twitter.com/HarlequinBooks

HREVIEWS

THE WORLD IS BETTER WITH *Romance*

Harlequin has everything from contemporary, passionate and heartwarming to suspenseful and inspirational stories.

Whatever your mood, we have a romance just for you!

Connect with us to find your next great read, special offers and more.

f /HarlequinBooks
🐦 @HarlequinBooks
www.HarlequinBlog.com
www.Harlequin.com/Newsletters

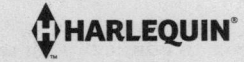

HARLEQUIN®

A *Romance* FOR EVERY MOOD™

www.Harlequin.com

SERIESHALOAD2015